PRAISE FOR
WINTER OF THE WOLF

"Martha's gut-wrenching and captivating story may be a work of fiction, but it hauntingly hits home. I felt like I was reading my worst nightmare."

—**Stephanie Ruhle,** NBC News

"Handler takes us deep inside one family's tragedy and shows us how our spiritual beliefs can guide us at our deepest moments of grief. As we travel with fifteen-year-old Bean through the loss of her beloved brother Sam, we see how friendship, trust, and deeply held beliefs help her navigate the painful aftermath of his death. In a mystery that races forward, Handler shows us the power of sibling love to endure forever."

—**Lisa Heffernan,** coauthor of *Grown and Flown: How to Support Your Teen, Stay Close as a Family, and Raise Independent Adults*

"All great books open our minds, broaden our visions, and strengthen our convictions, and Martha Hunt Handler's *Winter of the Wolf* does all three brilliantly. Much like a wolf, 15-year-old Bean follows her intuition, desperate and determined to prove her beloved brother did not choose to end his life. As readers follow her emotional and spiritual journey, they will, undoubtedly, begin to question their own beliefs about life and death and the interconnectedness of all spiritual beings. A breathtaking read from start to finish."

—**Hélène Grimaud,** founder of the
Wolf Conservation Center, world-renowned musical
artist, writer, and human rights activist

"A true literary masterpiece. Martha Hunt Handler takes us on an edge-of-your-seat thriller. We find ourselves arriving at the collision course between perceptions we've long held and deeper beliefs we've long ignored. While taking us on a journey of unfathomable pain, she asks us to ponder both the spiritual world around us and our interconnectedness to all souls who share the planet with us. You'll be awakened to the idea that the light that shines within us is too bright to ever be extinguished."

—**Wendy Diamond,** best-selling author,
TV personality, animal advocate, and founder of
Women's Entrepreneurship Day

"Let *Winter of the Wolf* take you on a journey of the soul to unearth the truth to set you free."

—**Emme,** supermodel and social reformer

"*Winter of the Wolf* is a compelling, heartfelt tale based on a story close to the author's heart. She takes what is a difficult subject and weaves a captivating story about life, death, grief, and gratitude. A must-read for any age."

—**Mary Ellen Keating,** former Senior Vice President of Communications for Barnes & Noble, Inc.

"What we attempt to capture in our photographs, Martha Hunt Handler portrays with her words in a heartbreaking story that reminds us of our interconnectedness with all that is living and breathing on our planet."

—**Paul Nicklen and Cristina Mittermeier,** cofounders of SeaLegacy, world-renowned nature photographers, and filmmakers

"Heartwarming and unflinching, *Winter of the Wolf* explores one family's struggle to face the complex nature of death and loss. A timely and important tale for all ages, it offers a powerful message of hope for our lives."

—Kristen Wolf, best-selling author of
The Way: A Girl Who Dared to Rise

"*Winter of the Wolf* takes you on an amazing and emotional journey through suicide and spiritual discovery."

—Bria Neff, teen wildlife artist and advocate

A NOVEL

WINTER
OF THE
WOLF

MARTHA HUNT HANDLER

GREENLEAF
BOOK GROUP PRESS

Published by Greenleaf Book Group Press
Austin, Texas
www.gbgpress.com

Distributed by Greenleaf Book Group

For ordering information or special discounts for bulk purchases, please contact Greenleaf Book Group at PO Box 91869, Austin, TX 78709, 512.891.6100.

Design and composition by Greenleaf Book Group
Cover design by Greenleaf Book Group
Cover image: "Canis Lupus" by Erik Fremstad

Publisher's Cataloging-in-Publication data is available.

Print ISBN 978-1-62634-718-2

eBook ISBN: 978-1-62634-719-9

Part of the Tree Neutral® program, which offsets the number of trees consumed in the production and printing of this book by taking proactive steps, such as planting trees in direct proportion to the number of trees used: www.treeneutral.com

TreeNeutral

Printed in the United States of America on acid-free paper

20 21 22 23 24 25   10 9 8 7 6 5 4 3 2 1

First Edition

My novel is dedicated to my mother, Peggy Hunt (1922-1994), Brendan Carey Flynn (1988–2001), Brendan's grandmother, Barbara Oehmke, and Brendan's mother, Gretchen Oehmke-Prudhomme, all of whom grounded me in my spiritual beliefs and encouraged me to seek out deeper truths.

"They say you die twice. One time when you stop breathing and a second time, a bit later on, when somebody says your name for the last time."
—**Banksy**

"Don't grieve. Anything you lose comes round in another form."
—**Rumi**

ONE

My first thought is that I might be dead.

I'm cold and stiff and I feel disoriented. If I'm not dead, then why am I lying on my back—something I never do—and why are the covers pulled *over my head*? I begin moving the fingers on my right hand slowly back and forth across the sheet, which feels somewhat reassuring. I slide my hand up along my body, brushing past my face before reaching out from beneath the covers. The frigid air startles me. I feel the top of my head and discover that my hair is partially frozen. Very odd.

Suddenly I hear voices in the distance. Gathering strength, I throw off the covers and force myself to sit up. Though every bone in my body aches as if I've been beaten, I exhale a huge sigh of relief. This isn't a morgue; it's my bedroom. It's freezing because I stupidly left my window open, which explains why I'm hearing these annoying voices. I slide over on my bed and reach to shut the window, and as I do, I notice that the water in the glass on my bedside table is frozen solid. Have I totally lost my mind? Why would I have left my window open in mid-November in northern Minnesota? Then I notice the blue hospital papers lying underneath the water glass and, in an instant, every horrific second of the previous night flashes through my mind: I'm likely sore because of how violently I was thrown around during our accident, and I opened my window because I thought I might be having a panic attack and hoped the cold air might snap me out of it. I was sweating, shaking intensely, and my heart was pounding like crazy. I felt lonely and scared. There was no one to help me. Mom was in shock, Dad was trying to console her, my two oldest brothers, Adam and Chase, would be totally useless, and my soul mate and favorite brother, Sam, was gone. As in *dead* gone.

The voices outside get louder, disrupting my thoughts. They seem somehow *unnatural*. How can life possibly go on without Sam in it? I push aside the curtains to see who's there. Down on the frozen lake, I see Billy Bishop, Mike Clayton, and Richie Branson, all junior varsity hockey stars, skating around something on the ice. I imagine that an animal has become frozen in the lake's surface. When the boys stop skating and begin poking whatever it is with their hockey sticks, I suddenly feel inexplicably outraged and oddly protective. Without thinking, I jump out of bed, run to the mudroom, slip into my winter boots, throw on my long down coat over my moose-print flannel pj's, put on a hat and mittens, and run out the door, down our backyard, and onto the ice, while screaming like a lunatic, "Stop! Don't touch it! Get away! Leave it alone!"

Their heads jerk up simultaneously, and they give me odd looks. They quickly skate away, though Richie swivels around to stare back at me for a second. It feels like an eternity. He's so incredibly hot with his curly auburn hair and piercing green eyes that normally I would have wanted to melt into the ice. I, and probably every freshman girl at my school, have a mad crush on him, but he must now think I've lost my mind. Or maybe he's already heard about Sam, as news travels fast in our small town, and he'll cut me some slack. I guess in the bigger scheme of things a cute boy no longer matters.

When I finally look down at the ice to see what it was they were poking, I find a beautiful young doe, which from her size I'm guessing is a yearling, lying in the area we all refer to as the black hole, the one spot in our neighborhood lake that always freezes last, due, we suppose, to an underground spring. This doe looks strangely ethereal, peaceful even, as if she's not deceased but simply resting on the ice. This is odd because the other animals I've seen frozen in our lake—and there've been many over the years—have had horribly panicked looks on their faces and their limbs were contorted into unnatural positions from their struggle not to succumb to drowning. Her left cheek, eye, ear, muzzle, and a small part of her neck lie exposed while the rest is frozen beneath the lake's surface. Her whiskers are especially cute. Each individual hair is coated in ice, which reminds me of a porcupine I made in kindergarten by sticking toothpicks into a potato.

I remember this art project for what it taught me: even a plain brown potato could develop its own character with the simple addition of a few well-placed toothpicks. This was important for me to understand because I was, at the time, experiencing major separation issues from Sam. Though he was two years older, we'd always been nearly inseparable. When we weren't together, I didn't feel quite whole. I wasn't sure if there was a me without him. The two years when he attended school and I didn't were excruciatingly difficult, at least for me. I'd been counting down the days until I could attend kindergarten. But what I hadn't fully grasped was that while we'd be at the same school, I wouldn't necessarily see him. Though his classroom was only five doors down from mine, there might as well have been an ocean between us. My teacher refused to let me visit him and we didn't even share the same lunch break or recess period.

Sam wasn't like other boys his age. He wasn't into violent video games or any electronics, for that matter. He didn't have any social media accounts. He hated guns and hunting. He'd sooner nurse an injured squirrel back to health than shoot it with a BB gun. He didn't particularly like watching or playing sports. He wouldn't cut his hair or wear nice clothes. What he did enjoy was being out in nature, and so did I. We spent as much time as we could outdoors, and we didn't care if it was below zero or if the sky was loaded with biting black flies.

But that fall, when he started second grade and I started

kindergarten, everything seemed to change. His class watched the movie *Nanook of the North*, and he became inexplicably mesmerized by the Inuit, an indigenous Arctic people. He'd always been drawn to Native Americans, but his interest in and admiration for the Inuit was even deeper. I think he'd probably been an Inuit in another life. That's the only explanation I have for his immediate and intimate connection with them.

The Inuit are people who live *with* nature, not separate from it. They hunt to survive but never for sport. They have respect for all souls and don't think of animals as being lower than us or soulless, and that was something Sam could relate to. From the time he was young, kids in our neighborhood called him "Indian boy" and "freak." I felt terrible when he got picked on, but I wasn't big enough or strong enough to stop it. Sam never seemed particularly bothered by their taunts. He was courageous and steadfast in his beliefs, even when it cost him popularity votes.

Around the time he became interested in the Inuit, he met Skip, and started spending most of his time either with his new best friend, or—now that he was beginning to read—with his head buried in a book about the Inuit. I felt abandoned. Maybe *fractured* is a better word. I guess I hadn't quite grasped that Sam and I were two individual souls. Looking at the doe's ice-coated whiskers, I struggle to remind myself of this lesson I learned so long ago.

I stare into the doe's big brown eyes, wondering what it is about her that has me feeling so bewitched. Then I notice paw prints circling her. They're embedded in the ice and much too large to be from a dog. Maybe a wolf made them. I follow the prints and note that they come from and trace back to the Enchanted Forest Island, which is located about a quarter mile from our backyard. On the island's shoreline, something black hastily retreats into the woods. It's hard to tell from this distance, but I believe it is a wolf or possibly a very large dog, though it doesn't resemble any dog in our neighborhood. Very strange. Wolves don't usually appear in broad daylight, and it's highly unusual for one to turn down a free meal; but it may have been scared off by the skaters.

Sam's big black-and-tan rescue hound, Dawg, comes bounding out of her dog door, running straight toward me. Instinctively, I move in front of the doe to block her. Dawg stops at my feet, sits, and looks up at me with eyes full of sadness and confusion. I take off my mittens and pet the top of her head and scratch behind her ears. Poor girl must be so confused. Does she understand that Sam's gone and not ever coming back? No, she couldn't possibly, because I can't believe it. I scratch her one last time, then bend down to kiss the top of her head before putting my mittens back on. She looks up at me and walks daintily around me to get closer to the doe. I'm about to chase her away, but I hesitate because I notice that rather than trying to eat it, as she's apt to do, she's actually licking its face. She honestly seems as bewitched with her as I am.

Wait! Could this possibly be the deer we collided with last

night? As it lay prone in the street in front of our car, we'd all assumed the deer was dead; its glassy eyes were vacant, it was bleeding out from a belly wound, and it was morbidly still. But maybe we were wrong, and the deer had survived. That would explain why Dad couldn't find any trace of her when he inspected the damage to his car. It would also explain Dawg's strange behavior. If this is that same deer, then she'd have picked up Sam's scent because he'd draped himself over its body.

"Away!" I command and point toward the shore. Dawg lifts her head, then lowers it and slinks away. When she reaches the shore, she dutifully sits down and stares back at me. Sam trained her very well. Not wanting to waste time, I quickly begin collecting the biggest rocks I can find along the shore and carefully place them in a large circle around the doe. Then I run up to our fishing shed and grab some leftover two-by-fours that are lying under a tarp and place them on top of the rocks to create a border. I don't yet know why this doe is important, but in the meantime, I don't want a wolf, Dawg, or anyone else disturbing her. I know this simple structure won't be much of a deterrent, but I figure it's better than nothing.

By the time it's complete, I'm freezing my ass off. My chest is starting to burn, and I'm quickly losing circulation in my hands and feet. Before I go, I gingerly step inside the barrier, kneel beside the doe, and gently touch her cheek. She's obviously dead, but she looks so alive that her cold, hardened face surprises me. I can't help but wonder if this is how Sam's body feels, if he is at this very minute lying naked on a cold metal exam table with a white sheet draped over his body in a cramped refrigerated drawer in the hospital morgue. It's one thing to see such a thing in horror movies and on medical shows, yet quite another to imagine this fate for your beloved brother.

Far in the distance, I hear a lone wolf howling. I'm confused and so is Dawg. I watch her stare in the direction of the howl, tilting her head nearly horizontally, first one way and then the other. Then she begins to howl. She's part hound dog so this isn't unusual, but there's something distinctly different about the pitch she's using. It's more sorrowful than normal. I guess we're both a bit weirded out that we're hearing a wolf at this time of day. Normally, because they're crepuscular, we only hear them between dusk and dawn. Weirder still, there's only one—a long, mournful howl from a lone wolf. I'm guessing it got separated from its pack during last night's storm and is desperate to rejoin them. Wolves were one of Sam's main totem animals, and hearing this howl suddenly reminds me of something he told me about how he wanted to be buried. I need to tell my parents before it's too late.

I enter the kitchen via the back door and immediately smell burnt toast. Dad is hovering over the coffee maker looking confused. His hair's a mess, his face is unshaven, and he's wearing an old, ripped, grey flannel robe. I rarely see him before he's showered and dressed, even on weekends, so his disheveled appearance is unsettling. He's not exactly fussy, but he does things in a certain order, and today he's totally out of whack. Then again, I ran out of the house like a crazed person in my pj's to chase off hot hockey players, so who am I to talk?

I unplug the toaster, remove the charred toast, and drop it into the trash. I turn around and notice that Dad's staring at me like I'm a ghost that's suddenly materialized before his eyes. "Where are you coming from?" he asks, frowning.

"The lake," I say without providing any further explanation.

He looks puzzled; I can tell he wants to ask me more questions but doesn't exactly know what to say. This isn't unusual; he rarely knows what to make of me. I toss my hat in a basket, take off my mittens, push them back into my coat pockets, remove my coat, hang it on a hook by the door, kick off my boots, and slide them under the bench. When I turn back around, he's still fumbling with the coffee maker. "Do you know how this dang thing works?" he asks.

I nod and take over, though I'm shocked at his ineptness. He's an engineer, and he's never asked me for help with anything mechanical. When I'm finished programming it, I push the start button and move over to grab a mug from the shelf behind his head, but he doesn't move out of my way. It's like he doesn't see me, like he's somewhere far, far away. I'm scared for him, or maybe I'm just scared for myself. This all feels horribly weird and awkward, but I guess nothing will ever be the same now that we're missing one of the most important members of our tribe. Welcome to my new, fucked-up life.

When I can't stand the silence another second, I ask, "How's Mom doing?"

He slowly looks in my direction. "What? Did you say something?"

"Yeah. I asked how Mom was."

"She's still sleeping. Whatever they gave her last night was pretty strong. I suspect she'll be out for at least a few more hours."

Lucky her. I'd give anything to be asleep, preferably for the rest of my life. But unfortunately, I don't have that luxury. I have to tell Dad about Sam's burial wishes, but I don't know how to bring up such a sensitive subject at such a difficult time. Then I remember the hospital papers lying on my nightstand, entitled "Patient Deaths and Next Steps," that I'd ended up with because my parents had refused to accept them. The hospital social worker said they contained information about our options for the handling and transportation of Sam's body. Following the autopsy, which may have already happened, she said we'd need to make decisions fairly quickly. "Dad," I say, "I have those papers from the hospital. Should I go get them?"

He nods, but his gaze remains fixed on the kitchen floor.

When I return, he's still in the same position. I hand him the papers, and he absently takes them from me, picks up his mug, walks to the kitchen table, plops down, takes his reading glasses out of his front pocket, puts them on, and starts reading. I make myself hot tea and sit beside him. When he's finished reading, he places the papers back on the table, removes his glasses, and tosses them on top. His face is expressionless. I so badly want to run back to my room to escape this painful silence, but for Sam's sake, I force myself to speak up.

"Dad?"

"Yes?"

"Sam really wanted a natural burial. Do you think we can make that happen?"

He looks up at me and frowns. "What the *hell* are you talking about?"

"You know, because of his Inuit beliefs. He wanted his body to be left out in the open so he could quickly become part of the food chain again. But I'm guessing that's not legal in Minnesota. If it isn't, then he wanted to be put in a burial pod, or at the very least have as green a burial as possible."

Dad lowers his voice and stares at me. "Bean, are you telling me that Sam talked about *dying*?"

Quickly understanding the implications of what I've said, I shake my head. "No. I mean, yes . . . but in a general way. He didn't want to be put into a casket or be buried in any way that's harmful to the environment. That's all he said."

"That's not . . . no," he says defiantly before standing and strolling out of the room, and I'm left to ponder if I've revealed too much. Does it mean anything that Sam talked about dying? I don't want to think so, but I can't be absolutely positive. I guess most kids don't spend much time wondering what will happen to their bodies after they die, but then again, Sam wasn't most kids. Though he'd only attended one funeral, it was enough to get him thinking about our arcane and environmentally disastrous burial practices.

These death discussions began shortly after my maternal grandma suffered a fatal heart attack, nearly five years earlier. Sam and I were around twelve and ten at the time, and we both accompanied Mom to Pennsylvania to plan and attend Grandma's funeral. And my older brothers, Adam and Chase, who were fifteen and thirteen, stayed home with Dad because all three of them had a horrible stomach bug.

After landing in Philadelphia, we rented a car and drove straight to the funeral home. The experience was beyond depressing. Mom was still in shock, and the mortuary guy was putting on the hard sell, making her feel bad about choosing an "inferior" casket, as if my deceased grandma, the most frugal woman I'd ever known, would somehow be offended. I remember looking over at Sam during the sales pitch and watching the blood drain from his face. I'm sure everything from the cheesy, satin-tufted lining to the split-top viewing lids and the clunky hardware was making him feel ill. He held it together for Mom's sake, but I could tell inside he was seething, because it was all so artificial, unnecessary, and tacky.

When we returned to Minnesota, Sam immediately started researching burial options, and a few days later he showed up in my bedroom with a bunch of articles he'd printed off the internet.

"Bean, you wouldn't believe how bad it is to bury someone the way Grandma was buried." He read from his papers: "'Every single year, in the US alone, burials require felling thirty million board feet of wood, ninety thousand tons of steel, and eight hundred thousand gallons of embalming fluid, which contains a toxic mixture of formaldehyde, glutaraldehyde, methanol, and a whole host of other solvents. It's a total nightmare. It's not only disrespectful to the soul, it's horrible for the planet."

"Do you want to be cremated?" I asked.

"No, that isn't natural either, and it's equally as damaging to the planet. It results in emissions of dioxin, hydrochloric acid, CO_2, and a bunch of other crap."

"Just tell me what you want, Sam," I said, quickly losing my patience.

"I want to be buried like an Inuit."

I shrugged, tilted my head, and raised my palms, code for "WTF, Sam?" He forgot that I didn't share his love for all things Inuit— that I hadn't memorized their customs, nor would I ever care to, and that every single thing I knew about them, he'd taught me.

"They bind the dead person's body with cords, wrap it in deerskin or sealskin, and expose it to the open air so it can decompose naturally. Doesn't that sound way better than being filled with chemicals, put in some creepy, claustrophobic casket, and lowered six feet into the ground?"

"I guess, but is that legal? I've never heard of anyone doing anything remotely like that around here."

"Good point. If it isn't possible, then just give me a green burial."

"A what?" I asked.

"It's when they put your body either into a biodegradable box or directly in the ground."

"Are you sure that's legal?"

"No, not in Minnesota. The closest state that allows it right now is Ohio."

Wanting this whole discussion to be over, I said, "Okay, I promise I'll do my very best to make sure you're buried the most natural way possible." As a joke, I added, "But you aren't planning on dying anytime soon, are you?"

Sam smiled and ruffled my hair with his hand. "Not when I still have so much left to teach you."

Remembering this conversation makes me want to scream on so many levels. First of all, I guess I should have asked Sam how he thought I'd get his body all the way to Ohio. But since we were talking theoretically, I figured it didn't matter. He was just a boy making sure his wishes were known. *Right, Sam?* And what about all the shit you needed to teach me? Do you honestly think you've already taught me everything I need to know? Because I can promise you, you didn't. I don't know shit about anything. In fact, I feel like I know less than I did before you died. And if you had nothing to do with your death, as I'm praying is the case, then I'm sorry for lashing out at you. But instead of feeling sad, I mostly feel mad, and my anger is directed at you. How could you be gone? How could you have left me?

The casket conversation wasn't the last one we had about death. About six weeks ago, Sam presented me with updated burial information. "Bean, look at this," he said, handing me more printouts. "This company in Italy makes burial pods that transform your body into nutrients that allow a tree to grow on top of you."

He showed me an illustration of a dead person lying in the fetal position inside an egg-like crate, which was buried underground. A large tree was growing above it. "Is this for real?" I asked.

"Yeah. Isn't it cool? Instead of destroying a forest, you act as fertilizer to help create one. Imagine a world with no more stupid cemeteries and lots more forests."

"That would be pretty cool," I admitted.

At the time, I didn't give this new information a second thought. I figured he probably had Google Alerts set to natural burials or something similar and was sharing it because he thought it was interesting. But now? Can I really be absolutely positive that there wasn't more to it? That he wasn't prewarning me? *No.* I will not go down this path. I must focus on the present. And what I feel presently is that I'm letting Sam down. I made a promise to him that I can't keep. Dad has to make a decision today about burying his *son,* and as much as I want to honor Sam's request, I can't make this any harder than it already is. I just pray that wherever Sam is, he understands and will find a way to forgive me.

On my way back to my bedroom, I walk by the den and see Adam and Chase sprawled on the furniture, peacefully sleeping, though I don't see how this is possible, given that at six feet, two inches each, they've had to contort themselves to fit on the sofas and, more importantly, the fact that their *brother is dead*. Do they not give a shit?

Farther down the hall I see that the boys' bedroom door is shut. Stretched across it there's yellow tape that reads "Police Line—Do Not Cross." We've been instructed not to enter it until the detectives have concluded their investigation. If only it could be sealed up forever. My brothers have no idea how lucky they are. They weren't here last night, so they have no visual of the chaos and associated horrors that took place in there. They were spared hearing Mom's horrifyingly primal screams, seeing Sam's lifeless, discolored body, and watching the EMTs' frantic and brutal attempts to resurrect him.

None of it made sense; it still doesn't make sense. I stare at their door for a minute and wonder what might lie behind it. What *happened* to my beloved brother? Will the detectives find any clues that will help explain why he's dead, and if so, will that information help ease my guilt and confusion, or only further crush me?

TWO

I f I tried to remember the nitty-gritty details of any other day in my life, I'd likely fail miserably. But each moment of the day Sam died seems to have been permanently etched into the folds of my brain. I woke up that morning feeling uneasy; something was off. This feeling hasn't come over me often, but when it has, something terrible has followed. For example, I knew my grandma died at least a couple of hours before Mom told me, I knew my dog Snoofy had been run over by a car before the doorbell rang, and I knew Sam had been seriously hurt falling out of a tree before I heard the ambulance in the distance. On each of these occasions I felt a sense of dread, and when I closed my eyes, I started getting visual flashes—sort of like video snippets—of what was going to happen.

But the day Sam died was different. I felt the dread, but I had no clear picture of what was going to happen or whom it might involve. I sat in bed for a few extra minutes that morning after my alarm went off and took deep breaths to try and get clarity about why I was feeling so awful, but no answers were forthcoming. Hoping to settle my stomach, I went to the kitchen to make myself some tea.

Chase and Sam were sitting at the table finishing their breakfast when I walked in. Though we all attend the same high school, they were going in early because Chase was seeing a math tutor and Sam had a week's worth of before-school detentions. I can't remember what these detentions were for, but it couldn't have been serious, because otherwise he'd have also been grounded, and he wasn't. They both gave me a curious look, because I normally woke up and headed straight to the shower. With the three of us sharing one bathroom, our mornings followed an exact routine, and I had broken it by appearing in the kitchen before I'd showered.

While waiting for the water to boil, I turned to Chase. "Are you driving?" I asked. Dad often let the boys drive our old Volvo to school.

He nodded while chomping on a mouthful of cereal.

"Drive safely," I said.

"Always," he said, sarcastically smirking.

Sam stood up to put his bowl and spoon in the dishwasher. He put his arm lightly over my shoulder. "Everything okay?" he whispered.

I shrugged. "I honestly don't know, but I don't feel right." Before I had time to explain, Chase placed his bowl in the sink and yelled, "Let's go, bro!" Sam blew me an air kiss on his way out, and I pretended it landed on my cheek.

The strange, anxious feeling stayed with me all day. I jumped every time they made an announcement over the school's loudspeaker, and I listened intently in the hallways to nonsense I normally would have ignored. When the final bell rang without my having been summoned to the office, I thought I'd feel relieved, but no such luck. When I arrived home, a note with my name on it was lying on the kitchen counter.

> *Bean—I'm off to the emergency room with Mrs. Zimmerman, who collapsed on her front steps. Dad and I are hosting the Daytons and Goodmans for dinner tonight, and I need your help. Please set the table and vacuum and dust the living and dining rooms. I'll call as soon as I know what's what.*
>
> *Love, Mom*

She had written another note for my brothers, pointing out that there was fresh rye bread, deli meats, and cheeses for sandwiches. So typical: I got put to work while my brothers were catered to.

As I was setting the dining room table, Mom called to tell me Mrs. Zimmerman had broken her hip but was stable, and she was waiting for Mrs. Zimmerman's daughter to arrive at the hospital. I felt bad for the old lady, but I knew her accident wasn't what had me feeling out of sorts.

About an hour later, Mom walked through the door, just as I begrudgingly finished the last of the chores. Without so much as a thanks, she frantically began pulling food out of the refrigerator while barking additional orders at me. Further adding to the tension was the fact that Dad, who'd promised he'd be home early to help, had left a message that his return flight from a three-day business trip to Chicago had been delayed due to a potential ice storm moving through our area. I hadn't heard about the storm, but they happened fairly frequently, so I wasn't worried. But when I looked outside, I thought the sky looked particularly dark and ominous, considering it was only a few minutes after four. Hearing Dad's voice on the answering machine didn't make me worry about him, but I began to feel less sure about the storm itself. He finally walked in about an hour later, just as a snow shower began, a mixture of sleet, snow, and lightning—a strange combination, even for northern Minnesota. At about 5:30, while the three of us stood working side by side in the kitchen, the phone rang.

"Yes, this is she," Mom said. She sounded polite but I could tell from the deep frown lines that suddenly formed between her brows that she was either annoyed or angry or maybe both. She nodded as if she were collecting information. "I'm sure there must be a reasonable explanation. Why don't I speak to him, and when I have all the facts, I'll get back to you? Thank you for alerting me to the situation."

I had no doubt, and I'm sure neither did Dad, that the call was from a teacher and involved Sam. IQ-wise, Sam likely had the biggest brains in our family, but he often chose to use his smarts to connive and sweet-talk rather than follow the rules. Julie, my best friend, often said, "Sam's either going to be the president of the United States or the leader of a drug cartel."

Mom had a large blind spot for Sam. And if I'm being perfectly honest, so did I. We tended to take his side and make excuses for him. However, in this instance, that wouldn't be possible because Dad was standing beside her, waiting for an explanation.

"That was Sam's English teacher," Mom said. "He hasn't turned in a paper that counts for a third of his semester grade. I'm sure there's a simple explanation. He probably completed it but neglected to hand it in. Let me see what he has to say for himself."

She turned to walk toward his room, but Dad stepped in front of her. "*I'll* talk to him. You know perfectly well you're not capable of disciplining that boy, which is why he thinks he can get away with crap like this."

"That's not fair," Mom countered. "This is serious. If he hasn't finished the paper, I promise you that he won't leave this house until he has, but I'd like to be the one to tell him."

I knew exactly what Mom was doing. She was trying to run interference. Sam and Dad often butted heads, and even minor disagreements had a tendency to escalate. I quickly veered into my room to avoid the inevitable family scene, but moments later I heard loud voices emanating from the boys' room, and from the sounds of it, I deduced Mom hadn't backed down. I immediately felt sick for Sam because it was his best friend Skip's eighteenth birthday, and they'd been planning his party for months. If the paper hadn't been written, which was probably the case, he wouldn't be going anywhere that night, which would not go over well.

Julie texted to ask if someone could pick her up. She was sleeping over, and she'd promised her parents, who'd gone out of town for the evening, that she wouldn't walk over unless the lightning had abated, which, from the sounds of it, it hadn't. I considered suggesting we have our sleepover Saturday night instead, but my sense of dread was still looming large, and I wanted her by my side. Adam was home for the weekend from college, but he and Chase weren't around, and I presumed Sam couldn't leave, so I asked Mom, who looked at me as if I'd requested that she run around the house naked.

"Bean, for God's sake, can't you see how busy I am? It will be a miracle if I can pull off everything before our guests arrive. You can ask your dad, but I doubt he's in any better position." As expected, he also declined.

When Julie texted again, I went to Mom with tears in my eyes (I was good at conjuring them up when necessary), and reminded her that I'd been helping her all afternoon. Could she please do me this one little favor that wouldn't take but ten minutes of her precious time? Though she claimed she felt bad, the answer was still no, so I asked if she would allow Sam to take me.

She said Dad had insisted that Sam not leave the house under any circumstances, but their guests were due to arrive any minute, so if we hurried and were discreet—by which she meant we should leave and enter via the garage and make sure the coast was clear—it was okay with her.

I knocked on Sam's door, and when he didn't respond, I called his name.

He opened the door, and I very quickly explained my situation.

"It's not happening," he told me, but I begged and pleaded with him, describing how tortuous my day had been. Eventually he relented.

We grabbed our coats and walked out to the garage. To my surprise, Sam walked directly to Dad's prized possession, a candy-apple-red '68 Mustang, opened the driver's door, and hopped in. *No one* was allowed to drive the car unless Dad gave his express permission, which *never* happened. I hesitated as I weighed the risk of stating the obvious, but I selfishly decided it wasn't worth pissing Sam off any more than he already was.

As soon as we pulled out of our driveway, I sensed I'd made a terrible mistake. The storm had kicked into high gear, and the snow showers had turned into blinding sleet. I guess I'd been too distracted helping Mom to notice how truly treacherous it'd gotten. I turned on the radio to diffuse the tension. Dad always had the radio set to some oldies station that mostly played songs from the sixties and seventies. We gave him shit for this, but secretly, we liked the music. "I Can See Clearly Now" sung by

Johnny Nash came on, which I thought was pretty funny, given how bad the visibility was. Sam, however, didn't seem amused.

Despite the ever-tightening feeling in my stomach, I tried to convince myself that everything would be okay. We were only going twelve blocks round-trip. What could possibly go wrong? But it was especially bad out, even for northern Minnesota. In less than three blocks, a thin layer of ice had begun forming along the edges of the windshield. Though the wipers were set on the highest speed, the area they kept clear of ice was diminishing by the second. Sam was sitting bolt upright in his seat, which told me that he, Mr. Daredevil himself, was scared. Halfway to Julie's house he turned off the radio. Even mellow Johnny Nash was a distraction in these conditions.

Julie was waiting for us on her covered front porch. As she made her way to the car, Sam dashed out to scrape ice loose from the wiper blades and around the edges of the windshield where the wipers didn't reach. I pushed open my door for Julie, and she squeezed in beside me on the small bucket seat. I figured three sets of eyes on the road were better than two. We both buckled into the flimsy seatbelt, Sam returned, and off we went.

He took the slightly longer route home, presumably so he could drive past Skip's house. Though it was early, the garage door was open, and a few of their friends were already moving things around to make room for the band equipment. Sam pulled into the driveway and put the car in park. "I'll be back in a sec," he said.

We watched him approach the guys in the garage. They stood around talking for a bit, and it looked like Sam helped connect a wire or two on a speaker. The longer he talked, the more my stomach lurched and my body stiffened.

"Bean, what's wrong?" Julie asked.

I explained that Sam had been grounded, and he wasn't allowed to leave the house.

"He can't go to Skip's party?" Julie asked.

"Nope."

"That sucks. He must be bummed."

"Oh, trust me, he is," I said.

"I know we talked about spying on Skip's party, but this weather is so bad, do you want to just hang out and watch a movie instead?"

"Yeah, I don't think we should go anywhere. I've been super anxious all day. I feel like something really bad is going to happen."

"Like what?" Julie asked, frowning.

"Wish I knew," I said, rubbing my shoulder against hers. "Sam's already been grounded so there's not a whole lot more Dad can do to him. But he wasn't supposed to leave the house and definitely not in this car, so we'll need to be very quiet and sneaky when we get back to my house."

Julie hugged me. "No problem, and everything's going to be okay. Don't worry."

Sam finally returned to the car about fifteen minutes later, though it felt like an eternity. We pulled out of the driveway and headed home. With only one more block to go, I began to feel even worse. Why was my heart beating so fast? To divert my thoughts, I turned toward Julie. "Are you okay with ordering pizza?"

"Sure, but I thought we were going to make homemade spaghetti?"

"Mom's so crazy cooking for her dinner party, we'll need to steer clear of the kitchen."

"Got it. Pizza is fine with me. What movie should we watch?" Julie asked.

"Thinking it's a great night for a horror flick."

"Yes! How about *Practical Magic*?"

"Perfect. It's been too long. We're way overdue."

Sam slammed on the brakes and the car slid sideways across the road. He frantically yanked the steering wheel one way and then the other, but the car wouldn't respond. Instinctively, I threw my arm across Julie's chest. We hit something hard in front of us. A second later, we hit something else even harder, which instantly crushed in the passenger's door, shattered the window by Julie's head, and forced her onto my lap. Secured only by the flimsy waist belt, our upper bodies jerked violently forward, and our heads smashed together as glass from the passenger side window sprayed across our bodies before the car finally stopped.

I struggled to speak. Sam banged on the steering wheel with both hands and screamed, "Fuck!" He took a big deep breath and turned to look us over. "You guys okay?" he asked. We nodded, and before we could say anything, he opened his door and dashed outside.

I was totally confused. I had no idea what we'd hit because it was so dark and at least one headlight was no longer working, and also because the wipers had stopped, and the windshield had instantly coated over in ice. We were carefully picking glass shards out of each other's hair and off our laps when we heard a strange primal moaning. We looked at each other, trying to imagine what was happening.

"Let's get out," Julie said, motioning toward Sam's open door.

I used my sleeve to clear away the remaining pieces of glass from the console, then carefully slid over the gear shaft and into the driver's seat. Before exiting, I pulled my hood over my head. The wind was howling through the trees and a sleety, hail-like mixture was bouncing loudly off the car, yet neither of these noises could begin to drown out Sam's eerie, mournful howls. I grabbed Julie's arm to help her out, and together we raced to the front of the car. The car was wedged into a large pine tree on the passenger's side and the front driver's side was also badly smashed. Illuminated in the dangling left headlight beam was Sam, shirtless and draped over the bleeding belly of a deer.

The deer's eye was open, but it was opaque and perfectly still. My mind quickly reeled back to Sam's Inuit beliefs surrounding the taking of another soul. I remembered that the first time you killed an animal for sustenance you had to mix your blood with that of the animal's as a show of respect to their soul. But what if the animal wasn't killed for sustenance? From the deep cries emanating from Sam, I understood that such a thing was probably taboo, and on his behalf, I felt truly sick. "It was an accident, Sam," I shouted. "You couldn't avoid hitting it. You're not responsible." My words didn't reach him.

A crack of lightning hit so close to us that we could feel the ground shaking. Without speaking, Julie and I rushed to either side of Sam, pulled him to his feet, and dragged him toward our house. He was reluctant to leave the deer, but I kept yelling, "Come on, Sam! Come on!" Finally, he stopped resisting.

I threw open the front door to our house and we staggered in, Julie and I supporting Sam between us. We landed in the entryway to the living room where my parents and their friends sat having cocktails. Their heads shot up, and they quickly looked us over before their eyes landed on Sam. Following their gaze, I saw why. His bare chest was covered in blood, and down the middle there was a long, straight, bleeding gash that ran from his sternum to his belly button. His eyes were glazed over and he was staring into space, as if he were an alien who'd just been beamed down to earth and hadn't a clue where he was or how he'd gotten here.

Mom flew off the sofa and ran to him. "My God, are you all alright? What happened?" She took his hand and quickly led him down the hall to the bathroom before we could explain.

Dad approached us, stopping directly in front of me. He took my head in his hands and jerked it up to face him. "What the hell happened?" he asked. "Where were you?" He looked as mad and confused as I'd ever seen him.

"We picked up Julie and got in an accident on the way back."

His features slackened the tiniest bit, as he quickly began to look us over. "Oh, Jesus. You're both okay? You aren't hurt, are you?"

I nodded, which wasn't easy given the headlock he still had me in. "We're alright, but we're freezing and drenched."

He let go of my head, but when we turned to leave, he said, "Wait, what happened to Sam? Where's his shirt, and how did he get that cut?"

"It's an Inuit thing. We killed a deer, and he was trying to appease its soul. But it wasn't his fault. The roads are really icy, and the deer came out of nowhere."

"Christ. Where did this happen? Where's the car?" Dad demanded.

"Across the street in front of the Temples' house. But it's not drivable, because we also hit a tree."

"Oh, hell," he said as he grabbed his winter coat from the front hall closet.

After we dried off and changed clothes, I left Julie in my room and went to the bathroom to check on Sam. Mom had cleaned him up and was busy bandaging his wound. His demeanor scared me. His face looked vacant and I could tell that he hadn't even registered my presence.

A few seconds later, Dad appeared in the bathroom. He

grabbed Sam by the shoulders and yelled, "What the hell were you thinking taking my Mustang? You were *grounded*. You were not to leave this house under any condition and certainly not in my car. You're just a hellishly reckless boy, and you always have been. For God's sake, you could have all been killed. You don't give a damn about anyone but yourself."

I tried to intervene, to explain that it was my fault and not Sam's. "Stay out of this, Bean. I'm talking to Sam. I'll hear your side of things when I'm done with him." I backed up but remained in the hallway, just out of his sight. "Is his cut serious?" he asked Mom. "You know it was self-inflicted, right?"

"He'll be okay," she said, "but you need to calm down. You're only making everything worse. Besides, if anyone's to blame for this mess, it's me. I told Bean that Sam could drive her to pick up Julie. Yell at me if you want to, but leave Sam out of it."

"Stop babying him," Dad growled. "My Mustang is totaled. Nothing more than a hunk of twisted metal thanks to him."

"That's what you're worried about? Your precious car?" Mom shouted. "We should be thanking our lucky stars that none of them were seriously hurt." She lowered her voice. "What happened, anyway? What did they hit?"

"Bean claims they hit a deer, but there's no deer anywhere near the car," Dad said. "My guess is Sam made up the deer story to explain why he hit the tree. Anyway, he looks perfectly fine, so why don't you get back to our guests. I'm going to talk to Bean for a minute, then I'll join you."

"Dad, I'm right here," I said, poking my head around the bathroom door.

"Let's talk in your room," he said. He turned back to Sam. "Make sure this mess is cleaned up. I'll talk to you later, but let me assure you that this is far from over."

Dad followed me back to my room. Julie was sitting on my bed, toweling off her hair. He took a deep breath. "Okay, girls, I want you to tell me the whole truth and nothing but. You're not in any trouble. I just want to understand exactly what happened."

His demeanor scared me. He looked totally enraged; his face was tight and red, and he looked taller and more menacing than I'd ever seen him. I had to struggle to remain calm as I explained what I thought had happened. When I'd finished, Dad completely lost it. "Goddamn it, Bean. There was no deer. Do you hear me? I found Sam's coat and shirt lying in the road in front of the car, but there was no deer. Was he going too fast? Is he stoned? Is that why he hit the tree? You need to help me understand what happened. Stop protecting Sam and tell me the truth for once."

I was too stunned to speak, plus I couldn't imagine what he was accusing me of. "I *am* telling the truth. There *was* a deer. It was dead and lying in the road, right in front of the car. We both saw it," I said, looking over at Julie, who nodded in agreement. "You saw all the blood on Sam's chest. Some of it was his, but most of it was from the deer."

"Then explain why it isn't there now. Did it just up and vanish into thin air? What I'm guessing is that Sam cut himself so your mother would focus on that and not the fact that he was driving recklessly and crashed my Mustang."

I defiantly shook my head. "No, Dad, it wasn't like that."

He grabbed me by the arm and squeezed. "You're a liar, just like your brother," he said. He dropped my arm and stormed out of the room.

I started shaking violently, and Julie looked equally shaken. Though Dad often lost his temper with the boys, he'd rarely so much as raised his voice to me, and he'd certainly never treated me roughly before. Equally confusing was what exactly he thought I'd done. Sensing Julie was even more upset than I was, I sat down on the bed and put my arm around her. "It'll all be okay," I said. "He's just mad that his fucking car is wrecked, and he's being a total jerk about it. That's what this is really all about."

"But the deer—"

"I know. It was dead, right? You saw it?"

Julie nodded, looking as confused as I felt.

Shortly after Dad walked out, Mom entered. "Are you girls sure you're okay?"

We nodded.

"I'd like you both to take two aspirin," she said as she opened the aspirin bottle and poured out four pills into her open palm and then handed us a glass of water. "You might feel alright now, but by tomorrow you'll likely be quite sore."

"Thank you," Julie said.

"You don't think you sustained a concussion or anything, do you? Were you wearing your seat belts? Did your heads touch the windshield?"

"We were wearing a seatbelt, and we didn't hit the windshield. We'll be fine. We're just shaken up."

"That's a relief. Before I leave you, I want to apologize for your father's behavior. I don't know if it's because of his car or because he thinks I betrayed him by allowing Sam to go out, but whatever the reason, he's not behaving rationally. Why don't you try and put this behind you and enjoy the rest of your evening? I know that's what I'm going to try to do." She turned to leave and then turned back around. "Julie, why don't you call your parents and let them know you were in an accident and that you're okay."

"They're out of town for their anniversary, and I'm totally fine. I think it would be best if I tell them tomorrow, if that's okay?"

Mom nodded.

Julie and I went into the den. I ordered our pizza, and we chose *Practical Magic* from Netflix. I thought about checking on Sam before we started the movie, but I figured that he probably just wanted to chill and not be bothered—especially by me, without whom this accident would never have happened.

When our pizza arrived, I went back to the boys' room to see if Sam wanted a slice.

"I'm not hungry," he said, without opening the door, which in hindsight was a tad strange. "Just save me a couple of slices for later."

"Okay," I said, lingering at his door. "I'm really sorry," I said, and when he didn't answer, I went on. "I never should have asked you to pick up Julie, but you know the accident wasn't your fault, right? You were driving so slowly and carefully. That deer came out of nowhere. No one could have avoided it." Silence. "When Dad went out there, the deer was gone. You didn't kill it. All you did was stun it. It has to be alive if it was able to walk away."

"Thanks, Bean," he finally said. "I'd like to believe you, but that deer wasn't going anywhere."

"Well, it did. Dad doesn't even believe we hit a deer. He thinks we made it up to explain why we hit the tree."

"Whatever. Dad's an asshole."

"Yeah, he is. Anyway, we're going to watch *Practical Magic* if you want to watch it with us."

"Can't. I've got a huge fucking paper to write before I can be released from my bondage."

"Well, if you need anything at all, we're in the den."

"Later," Sam said.

That was the last word he ever spoke to me: "Later."

I walked back to the den still feeling odd. I tried to shake it off, to convince myself that our accident was what had me feeling out of sorts all day, and since it was over, I could finally relax. But my sense of unease would not loosen its grip.

Half past nine or so, Julie and I paused the movie and brought our dirty plates and empty soda cans into the kitchen. Mom walked in behind us. "Would you girls be interested in making a little extra money by clearing the table and loading the dishes?"

Always up for making money, we agreed. I set the remaining four slices of pizza on a plate and put plastic wrap over it, then we cranked up the radio and got to work.

Mom came back as we were finishing up and asked us to make a pot of coffee and cut and serve the dessert. When she saw the plate I'd made for Sam, she asked how he was doing and if he'd had any supper.

"I think he's alright, but he hasn't eaten anything. He asked me to save him some slices for later."

She frowned. "That's not like him. He's always hungry. I bet your dad's dreadful behavior earlier upset him. Let me see if I can interest him in some of our leftover roast beef and potatoes before you put it away. He won't be able to resist that."

She walked down the hall with a prepared plate of food. A few seconds later, the screaming started.

The radio was on and the water was running in the sink, so at first Julie and I looked at each other, confused because we couldn't figure out where the horrific sounds were coming from—they barely sounded human, more like the anguished, mournful howls of a wolf caught in a foot trap. When Julie turned off the water and radio, it quickly became clear that the screams belonged to Mom and were coming from the direction of the boys' room.

All of us—Dad, the dinner guests, Julie, and I—reached the boys' room at about the same time. We found Mom slumped in the doorway, screaming and pointing across the room to the closet door. Following her gaze, I saw Sam's lifeless body hanging from a belt attached to their chin-up bar. His head and neck looked opaque and waxy, like something you'd see at Madame Tussaud's. I froze. My first thought was to run out of the room, as if doing so could somehow turn back time. It didn't occur to me to try and help Sam. I knew he wasn't there. Not even a faint trace of him still lingered in that room.

"Call 9-1-1!" Dad shouted to Mr. Goodman as he ran over and lifted Sam's body up to unhook the belt from around his neck. He gently laid him on his back on the floor and began performing CPR.

Racking sounds came from Sam's chest each time Dad blew into his mouth. I might have thought this was a good sign if I hadn't learned from watching an old episode of *House* that this was called a death rattle, nothing more than the sound of mucus being moved around one's chest when air is forced into their lungs. This coupled with the gruesome discoloration of his body—his arms were yellowish-green, his bare feet dark purple—left me with little hope that Sam had any chance of being resurrected. I immediately felt as if I'd been severed, like I was no longer whole.

Mom knelt on the floor beside Sam's head, opposite Dad, who was leaning over Sam from the other side. She stroked his hair away from his forehead. "You're going to be okay, Baby," she said. "You can't leave me. Please don't dare leave me, Sam." I stepped closer and crouched on the floor near his waist. I took Sam's limp right hand and raised it to my cheek. Cold and lifeless to the touch, it only further confirmed what I'd felt from the second I saw him: this body before us was nothing more than a shell. Sam was already long gone.

Outside, sirens screamed; there was shouting, and the room quickly filled with EMTs, firemen, and policemen. They pushed me roughly aside and quickly cut off Sam's T-shirt. Then they began working on him as if he were a rag doll and not a human being. I threw up in the trash bin beside Adam's desk. That's when I saw the camouflage belt lying on the floor. Even in the state I was in, there was something about it that didn't feel right. For one thing, it wasn't Sam's. He wouldn't have been caught dead wearing a belt clearly designed for hunters or someone in the military.

After what felt like an eternity—but I learned later from the EMTs' report had only been fourteen minutes—a decision was made to transport Sam to the hospital. Mom pleaded with the head EMT to assure her that Sam would be okay, but he wouldn't answer her or even look her in the eye. Sam was quickly loaded onto a stretcher and then wheeled out of the house and into the waiting ambulance. Mom clung to the back of the stretcher.

We were instructed to go to Mercer Memorial Hospital. Though Mom insisted on staying with Sam, they dismissed her, explaining they needed room in the ambulance to continue working on him. She was afraid to let him out of her sight.

Suddenly, I was too. I felt if he were taken away, it would be the point of no return. When the ambulance doors shut, Mom started pounding on them, but they paid no attention. Off they drove, with lights flashing and sirens blaring.

Dad had to forcibly drag Mom into the Goodmans' car, which Mr. Goodman had waiting for us on the street. The sleet had stopped, and the temperature had dropped drastically. I wasn't wearing a coat, and I remember feeling chilled to the bone walking to their car. When we drove past the wrecked Mustang, I stared at it in disbelief. It was hard to believe that our accident had taken place just a couple hours ago. It felt like it'd been weeks or even months.

We followed directly behind the ambulance, speeding through traffic lights and stop signs. None of us spoke. When we arrived at the ER, we jumped out of the car and stood by as the stretcher was pulled out and whisked down the hall. Mom tried to follow, but a woman appeared out of nowhere and guided us to a private waiting area. She began to rub Mom's shoulders and eventually got her to sit down on a sofa, though at no point did Mom's sobs abate. Seeing her in so much pain was even worse than seeing Sam's lifeless body. I wanted to hold her and tell her everything would be okay, but I'd never been a good liar. Dad sat beside her, and I plopped down on the floor at their feet and leaned my head against their legs, suddenly feeling the need to be physically touching them. When the attending physician finally came in to speak to us, he had a blank look on his face. You didn't need to be psychic to know what he was about to say.

"I'm so very sorry," he said, avoiding eye contact. "We did everything we could, but we weren't able to revive him. If you'll give us a few minutes, we'll have the room cleaned up and you can go in and say goodbye if you wish. A grief counselor will be out to talk with you shortly."

Mom's sobs quickly became screams, and she began to shake the doctor, as if she were trying to get him to take his words back. Dad got between them and put his arms around her and moved her away. The doctor didn't seem like he was the least bit fazed by her assault; it obviously wasn't the first time something like that had happened to him. Thankfully, our family physician, Dr. Marks, arrived a few minutes later and gave Mom a sedative. Dad, who appeared calm but strangely detached, asked me to sit with her while he had a word with our doctor and one of the policemen who was stationed outside the waiting room. I nodded, sat down next to her, and began to absently rub her back. A few minutes later Adam and Chase ran in, completely out of breath. Their eyes darted around the room. Dad was still occupied with Dr. Marks and didn't seem to be aware that they'd arrived, and Mom, slumped beside me, also didn't appear to know or even care that they were there.

"What's going on, Bean? What happened to Sam?" they demanded. "Is he okay?"

I let my hand fall from Mom's back. I slowly stood, looked

them in the eyes, and then my knees buckled, and I landed on the floor at their feet. There was something about seeing my brothers' somber faces that suddenly made the whole situation go from surreal to real in a split second. It had all been such a whirlwind of activity and craziness that I hadn't registered the fact that it was *really, truly* happening. That Sam was gone *forever*. That nothing I did from that moment forward could bring him back.

Adam and Chase quickly lifted me to my feet before setting me down in the sofa across from Mom. They sat on either side of me, and each took one of my hands in theirs. This simple act of kindness from my two brothers who'd rarely ever touched me opened the floodgates, and my tears began to flow uncontrollably. "He's gone," I said. "They couldn't bring him back."

Dad walked in and came over to stand in front of us. "There's nothing more we can do here. Let's all go home." Dad helped Mom to her feet, and my brothers pulled me up and out of the sofa. Just as we were about to leave, a hospital staffer emerged and asked to have a word with Dad. He nodded at Adam, who quickly stepped over to help support Mom. Thankfully, she was well out of earshot when the staffer whispered to Dad. "Your son's body will be sent for an autopsy shortly. Please read through this packet and call us tomorrow at your earliest convenience to let us know which funeral home you've chosen. We'll take care of everything else." She then reached out to hand Dad the papers. He just stood there, ignoring her. Reluctantly, I reached out and took the packet.

As the staffer turned to leave, the policeman reappeared. He whispered something in Dad's ear that I couldn't make out. As we made our way to the entrance, Adam and Chase took off their coats and put them around Mom and me before we all solemnly walked to our Volvo, which the boys had left running, with the doors wide open, in the Emergency entrance circle.

I guess Dad decided for all of us that we didn't need to see Sam's body one last time. I still don't know if this was a good idea or a bad one.

When we passed the Mustang on the street, Chase looked over at me with a questioning look, but I offered no explanation. When we reached the house, all the lights were on, the front door was wide open, and Louis Armstrong's "What a Wonderful World" was playing, a song I recognized from my parents' Spotify "entertaining" playlist. I thought, *It is definitely not a wonderful fucking world.* We walked through the front door in single file and made our way to our bedrooms. The carpeted hallways were filthy— muddy footprints everywhere. I felt like we'd been robbed and violated, which, in a way, we had been. Dad carefully removed the coat from Mom's shoulders, tossed it to Adam, and then took hold of her elbow and gently guided her into their bedroom. She was zombie-like. I followed close behind, but when I got to my bedroom door, I froze, unsure what to do. I saw my brothers slowly make their way back to their room, all the while staring at the footprints, as if trying to piece everything together. The boys stopped abruptly, and when I looked up, I saw why. Yellow crime tape was pulled tautly across their bedroom door. Before they could ask, Dad emerged from the master bedroom and carefully shut their door behind him. He waved the boys away from their door and then grabbed pillows and blankets from the hall closet and handed them to Adam and Chase. "We've been asked not to enter your room until they say otherwise. They'll be here in the morning to complete their investigation. Until then, take anything you need from my closet or the medicine cabinet and go sleep in the den."

"Dad, can you please tell us what happened?" Chase asked. I could tell he was totally confused, because as bad as the Mustang looked, it didn't look like the type of accident someone dies from. The windshield wasn't even cracked.

Dad nodded and pointed them toward the den. He sat with them and I heard him say that Sam had hung himself. And that is the story that everyone—except me—believed.

THREE

F our months have now passed, and I still don't understand how it all went down. If Sam did what they say he did, what the police and detectives called a self-killing, I'd know it to be true. *Wouldn't I?* After all, I knew him better than anyone, and I know for a fact that he would not intentionally leave me. Because here's the thing: Sam and I were supposed to be *together* in this life. In fact, he wanted me here so badly, he practically conjured me up.

When he was only two years old, he pointed to Mom's tummy and said, "Baby."

Before hearing Sam's announcement, she'd been positive that the few extra pounds she'd gained and her spotty periods were simply signs of early menopause, because, she later told me, she and Dad had decided their family was complete, and they were being very careful. But the moment those words came out of Sam's mouth, Mom knew.

Soon after his pregnancy proclamation, Sam began to talk

to me. He'd ask Mom to sit, then he'd move closer and whisper into her belly button. He also asked to see picture books showing how babies grow. He called me Bean almost from the start. Sam said I told him that was my name, but Mom wondered if it didn't have more to do with the drawings of developing fetuses he saw in those books. In either case, Sam won, because the name on my birth certificate, much to Dad's annoyance, is Bean Hanes.

Now the only place Sam still exists is in my dreams, which is blissful—until it isn't. One minute I'm floating along in some magical alternative reality, and the next I'm slammed back down into the dark depths of my earthly hell. It totally sucks, because my dream world and my real world are now light years apart.

In the dream I just awoke from, I'd been peacefully sitting in the front of our canoe enjoying a warm, misty morning, while Sam sat at the back, fishing and amusing me with Inuit stories. Suddenly, my end of the canoe rose, as if weight had been added to the rear. I jerked my head around in time to see Sam falling backwards out of the boat, as if in slow motion. Before I could laugh at his clumsiness, my dream sped up and from somewhere distant I heard the sound of Mom whimpering. Just like that, dream over.

I don't have to open my eyes to know Mom's slumped at the foot of my bed, but rather than rushing to comfort her, I lie perfectly still and feign sleep. Though my actions, or I guess I should say my *inactions*, might lead you to believe otherwise, I love Mom dearly. But after having spent the time since Sam's death desperately trying to comfort her, even though I really feel it's *her* job to comfort *me*, I have nothing left to give. I'm an empty vessel—exhausted and, apparently, devoid of compassion. In fact, all I feel for her right this minute is contempt. I know this sounds awful, but let me explain.

The only good moments I have nowadays are when I'm dreaming, because during that blissful time I don't know or can't remember that Sam is no longer with us. He's a part of my dreams like he always was, so when I'm awakened by the sound of Mom's heart-wrenching sobs, I can't help but feel that I've been robbed of the best part of my day before my feet have even touched the ground. And this is doubly true today, because it's my fifteenth birthday. Plus, I don't know how long I have left until my dream world catches up to my real world, and Sam is forever erased from both, but I'm guessing that all too soon I'll be living my nightmare 24-7.

If Sam were alive, I'd have woken up to find his birthday letter, telling me why I'm the most special sister in the whole world, slipped under my door. I got them every year, and they're the only gifts I really cared about. Last year his card read:

Happy Fourteenth Birthday Bean,

I know this card is supposed to be about you, but I have to be honest, you turning fourteen kinda sucks—for me. I seriously want you to slow down! I know this sounds like something a parent would say, but no joke, it's exactly how I feel. I'm not at all stoked about you becoming a freshman next fall. When we were in middle school together, I saw you as my tomboyish, headstrong kid sister who was always up for anything and everything. I barely thought of you as a female. You were simply my sidekick. I know that deep down, you're still you. It's just that suddenly there's this attractive young woman emerging.

Sometimes I look at you and barely recognize you—for real! This hit me recently when I was coming home on the late bus and we passed Woody Park and I saw you there hanging out with your friends. Then some guys sitting a few rows in front of me started talking about how hot you are. I can't really explain why, but I felt completely enraged. You're growing up and I know I have to accept that, but I'm just letting you know that it's going to be extremely difficult. And next year, when you're in high school, I'm sure it will be infinitely worse. But I promise that I will learn to chill, because I want you to enjoy yourself (to a degree!) without an overprotective brother stalking you.

But today is about you, not me. So, I will take this opportunity to tell you that you're the most perfect Bean that was ever created. You're smart, funny, creative, kind, and generous of spirit. I want you to remember this when you start to date, which will undoubtedly happen all too soon. (Here I go again!) Please don't ever settle, no matter what. I know most of the guys in our town, and, I assure you, none of them are good enough for you! But, unfortunately, I suppose you'll have to figure that out for yourself. Just promise me that no matter what, you'll always trust your instincts. Don't do stupid things just because your friends are doing them. You were given an exceptional brain and you must use it to its full advantage. I love you like no other. Enjoy this year and continue to cultivate your wisdom.

Your loving (and super-protective) brother,

Sam

Sam's cards always seemed to strike the perfect note, telling me exactly what I needed to hear in that moment. I remember reading this letter like it was yesterday. I'd woken up that morning feeling miserable and crampy. I went across the hall to the bathroom and quickly learned that not only had my period started, but three large zits had erupted on my forehead and right cheek. WTF? What kind of birthday bullshit was this? I didn't want to go to school looking like that, and I certainly didn't want to follow through on my evening birthday plans that involved meeting a bunch of my friends around five to go on a long hike before going to the annual spring school bonfire and dance. I decided to ask Mom if I could stay home from school so we could have a mother/daughter day. Knowing her, she'd likely agree. When I got back to my room, I noticed Sam's card sitting on my bed. I immediately got back into bed, pulled up the covers, and started reading. A few seconds later, I'd sprung out of bed and started getting dressed for school. Surely, a smart, self-assured woman wouldn't let a few blemishes ruin her birthday.

But now I'm fifteen and it feels like every birthday from now on will be ruined because I'll never get another birthday note from Sam.

I'm also angry that Mom, once again, has stolen precious moments of my zzz-time. As if my waking moments aren't horrendous enough, every time I put my head on the pillow, the *terrible* questions begin to swirl round and round in my head until I'm forced to turn on my bedside light to make them go away. I repeat this sequence over and over, night after night, until I eventually pass out from exhaustion. But by then it's well into the wee hours of the morning, so I generally wake up feeling more exhausted than when I went to sleep. And sleep is ultra-important, because although I'm the runt of our litter, I've somehow become our family's caretaker.

My oldest brother, Adam, who's twenty, is away at university, and Chase, who's eighteen, plays varsity hockey and is exempted from household chores, though I have no clue why. Mom, who used to be Supermom, is now worse than useless; she's super needy. Rare is the day when she manages to get out of bed *and* take a shower, let alone leave the confines of our house or even their bedroom. And Dad, well, he's an expert at texting me endless lists of chores to complete, but as far as I can tell, he seems to do very little himself. In fact, he's not around much these days. Honestly, I can't fault him. If I had somewhere to go, I'd be long gone, too.

Whoever said that "time heals all wounds" must have been smoking crack. Every day I feel heavier and angrier than I did the day before. Even something as simple as brushing my teeth takes a tremendous amount of effort. I feel like a tortoise slogging through quicksand. Where I once would have been excited to get to the other side, I'd now prefer to close my eyes and let the earth swallow me whole. I just don't give a shit about anything. I honestly don't see the point of living.

I'm still burrowed beneath my covers and feigning sleep when Mom finally leaves my bed and shuts my bedroom door. Going back to sleep no longer feels like an option, so I sit up to collect my thoughts. I'm feeling especially bleak today, probably because of my aforementioned birthday. Then I remember something my English teacher, Ms. Golde, suggested. Yesterday, while handing back a short story I'd written about Sam, she touched my shoulder and looked at me as if she could tell I was hanging on by a thread and needed reassurance that I mattered. I tried not to think about how sad it was that she could see how wrecked I am, but my own family doesn't seem to have a clue or even care. Anyway, she asked that I stay after class, and that's when she suggested that on days when I'm feeling especially low, I should focus on all the people who are keeping me tethered to the planet. Today my list includes:

Mom—I still love her, even if she's being a total slacker, plus it *literally* would kill her if I chose to off myself.

Dad—We aren't exactly close, but since Sam's death he's softened, and I pray that our shared grief will somehow help break down the walls that have built up between us over the years.

Julie—She was my soul sister until I broke up with her, or whatever it's called when you tell your best friend that you need to stop seeing her for a while.

Skip—Sam's best friend who's been mysteriously absent from my life since Sam left but whom I still have a mad crush on when I'm not busy hating on him for abandoning me in my most dire time of need. And BTW I'm not talking about some schoolgirl kind of crush like I have on Richie Branson, which is based entirely on looks, since I haven't spoken more than five words to him. What I'm talking about is that I believe, in the deepest part of my soul, that many moons from now Skip and I will be together, like forever. We get each other, and we get Sam, which is now imperative, because how could I be with anyone for all eternity who'd never even known Sam? Of course, Skip doesn't have a clue how I feel about him, but that's okay. Someday, when the time is right, he will. That is, if he ever resurfaces.

Dawg—Sam's dog isn't actually tethering me to anything, but if she's psychic, as I suspect dogs are, and she knows I've included her in this list, I hope it might stop her from hurling herself in front of the next car that drives by, which from the look of her is high on her doggy to-do list—if she can extract herself from Sam's bed long enough to do the deed.

Adam and Chase—I feel bad even thinking this, but in all honesty, my brothers tether me to the planet even less than Dawg. Sorry, guys, but you know it's true. But I do pray that sometime down the road, when we're all in a better spot, I'll discover that they're deeper than I give them credit for. Not likely, but I'm trying to be optimistic. Plus, if they discovered they weren't on my list, they'd be hurt and that is not my intention.

Albert Einstein and Virginia Woolf—This is probably confusing, since both are deceased and, therefore, if I did off myself, I'd probably have a better chance of seeing them on the *other side* than I do here. But I include them because they inspire me. Albert makes me want to believe there are dimensions to our universe beyond those I can see or even imagine, and Virginia helps me believe in the transformative power of words.

The Doe—If the doe frozen in our lake turns out to be the same deer we hit, then it will help restore my faith in my intuition.

Still perched in my bed, I hear a knock at my bedroom door, then Dad abruptly walks in.

"Jesus. Could you at least wait for me to answer before you come barging in?" I say.

"Your mom said you were still sleeping. Anyway, you need to get up," he says, motioning me out of the bed with a sweeping arm. "It's almost ten. I've left clean dress shirts that need pressing on the ironing board, Dawg needs to be fed, and afterwards go check on your mom and see if you can get her to eat something. I tried earlier, but she wasn't hungry. I'm leaving for the office now. Text me later, and we'll figure out dinner."

I don't acknowledge him or his demands because I notice that he has one hand hidden behind his back, and in my delusional state I imagine that it might be holding my birthday gift. When I don't immediately spring into action, he says, "What are you waiting for? Get up and get going, lazybones."

Lazybones? It's a Monday but we have the day off from school for parent-teacher conferences, which my parents won't be attending because I've managed to intercept both the email and the follow-up phone call. I figure things are bad enough without their hearing that my grades have slid from straight As to mostly Cs and Ds. Shouldn't I be allowed, on this rare day off, to try and catch up on my sleep? I want to scream, but I don't have the strength. When Dad turns to leave, I realize that his missing hand has simply been kneading his lower back. Chronic pain is the common thread now running through our lives; his is just a bit more localized than mine.

"Kill me now," I mutter under my breath.

"What?" he says, turning back around.

"Nothing," I say. It's not worth it.

After he closes the door, I pull the covers over my head and begin to wildly kick my feet. I might be fifteen, but I think it's official: I'm the biggest fool on the planet for believing that anyone in my pathetic family might remember it's my birthday, as if I or the anniversary of my birth remotely matter to anyone anymore. Okay, I'll admit it; I feel sorry for myself. Very, very sorry.

While still thrashing around, I feel a hand gently rub the top of my head. When I push the covers back, I'm startled to see Julie standing beside my bed, smiling down at me.

Julie became my ex-BFF a few days after Christmas, which was about six weeks after Sam died. At the time, I was living on autopilot. It was one gray day followed by another. I did only what was expected of me. I didn't have good days or bad days; they were all just meh.

"Happy birthday, Bean," Julie says. Her smile quickly becomes a frown and that, coupled with the way she's biting her lower lip, lets me know how shitty I look. For months I've been hiding under a large brown hoodie of Sam's. In the beginning, I wore it to shield me from the harsh words being muttered throughout the halls of our school about Sam and the circumstances of his death: "If he was so messed up, why didn't his family get him help?" "There was something off with that kid." "If you ask me, Sam Hanes was the definition of a freak." But later, after the hurtful words finally died down, I wore it because Sam's scent still lingered in its fibers, and I was desperate to savor every last molecule of him. Another benefit was that when I draped the large hood over my head, it helped hide how hideous I looked. Paired with sweatpants, I'd been able to morph into a ghost who was only masquerading among the living.

"Thanks," I say. As I readjust myself farther up in the bed, I catch a whiff of Julie's cucumber oil, her signature scent, and its familiarity nearly breaks my heart. She takes a deep breath and shifts uncomfortably. I would never have imagined that we could feel so awkward around each other, but there's no mistaking this feeling. We're strangers now, or more accurately, I guess it's just me who's *strange*.

"You okay? I mean, are you sick or something?" she asks, with a look of genuine concern.

I consider telling her I'm highly contagious so she'll leave, but I can't lie to her, so I simply shake my head. She looks so fresh and cute that it makes me want to puke. Her perfectly styled long black braids fall down the front of either shoulder, and she's wearing a lilac-colored sweater, ripped jeans, and high tan UGG boots, on which she's drawn daisies using fabric paint. Julie's the ultimate DIY-er.

"I'm okay. This is just me now," I explain, crossing my arms in front of me.

She nods and forces a smile. "I brought you a present." She walks over to my desk chair, lifts her down coat that's lying on top of it, and grabs a wrapped gift from beneath it, which she gives to me. "It's nothing special, but I thought you might like it."

She's wrapped the gift in a recycled plain brown bag, on which she's drawn funny pictures of raccoons, birds, rabbits, and bears roaming in a magical forest. I uncross my arms and carefully remove the paper, so I don't tear her artwork. Inside, I find a beautiful purple-leather-bound journal with lighter purple hand-stitching on the front that reads "My Journey."

"It's very cool. Thank you. Did you make it?" I ask.

Julie nods.

"Very impressive. You've gotten really good."

"Well, I've had a lot of time on my hands."

I know this is a reference to my blowing her off these last few months, which makes me feel worse than I already do.

"So, what're your plans for the day?" she asks.

I shrug.

"Okay, so let's do something."

"Like?" It's been so long since I've done *anything* that her suggestion sounds absurd.

"Whatever you want. It's *your* birthday. You decide."

"I only wish that was the case. Birthday or no birthday, I've got a lot of shit to do. For starters, I have to make Mom breakfast, try to get her to shower and dress, feed Dawg, deal with the laundry, and iron my dad's shirts. Then I should probably start on the shitload of homework that I blew off all weekend. No, make that all semester."

"I'm sorry, Bean. That's a bummer. But can't you take a few hours to celebrate?" Julie leans over and pushes my curtains aside. "Look at how amazing it is outside. The sun is out, the snow is sparkling, and for the first time since November it's supposed to be above freezing. You know how we always have that one magical spring-like day that makes us realize that winter won't last forever? Well, today is that day, so we have to celebrate."

I tilt my head and stare at her. "We at the Hanes household no longer celebrate birthdays or the change of seasons."

Julie frowns. "Well, that totally sucks."

"Life sucks. But back up. Why are you here? I—"

Julie sticks her hand out to cut me off. "You wanted space,

and I gave you space, but enough is enough. You need me, and I need you. That's how we roll." She nudges my shoulder, and I instinctively move over to make room for her beside me on my bed. She sits down and then reaches over and pushes aside some of the matted, greasy hair that's fallen in front of my eyes. "You have to admit that this self-imposed exile of yours hasn't exactly worked wonders. You look like shit, and as far as I can tell, you're in the same bad space you were in three months ago. No, actually, I'd say you're in an even worse space."

I nod. It would be pointless to object.

"What can I do to help?" Julie says. "Because you can't go on like this."

"Easy. Bring Sam back," I say.

She smiles. "Oh, Bean, you know I would if I could. Unfortunately, I'm not that powerful of a witch."

Hearing the word *witch* makes me smile just a tad, as it's another reminder of how deep our friendship runs and all the crazy things we've done together. Like the time in fifth grade when we decided to become witches. We went to our town library and checked out every book we could find on witchcraft. And what we were surprised to learn was that most witches were nothing more than herbalists who studied plants to determine their healing properties. I guess back in the day, people were incredibly fearful and skeptical, mostly because they didn't understand the causes of illnesses and diseases, so when these so-called *witches* were able to *cure* people, instead of being thankful, the people became suspicious of their powers and persecuted them.

Though Julie and I weren't particularly interested in plants, we were interested in knowing if we had any witch-like powers. Julie suggested we start with a love spell, because she knew I had a crush on a boy named Trevor Jones, who did not appear to be the least bit interested in me.

We came up with a random list of objects we thought would help make the spell work, such as one of his socks, something written in his own handwriting, one of his hairs, etc. Then we wrote out a ridiculously cheesy spell:

There is darkness, there is light,

It's time for Trevor and Bean to unite.

Let the wind howl and the moon be fully seen,

For this is when Trevor will have eyes only for Bean.

Surrender now, Trevor, and meet your fate,

For Bean will be your forever soul mate.

On the next full moon, we went to Julie's basement, lit a candle, put everything we'd collected into a bandana, and swung it around over our heads as we chanted our spell aloud three times. Lo and behold, two weeks later, Trevor passed me a note asking if I wanted to play tetherball at lunch. That experience coupled with a few other successful spells kind of freaked us out. We mutually agreed to stop being witches and promised ourselves we wouldn't resume until we had a worthy cause. We didn't want to have our powers revoked due to negligence.

"I don't get it. I mean, what the hell happened? How could Sam be gone? I'm still hoping that I'll wake up from this nightmare, but I know I never will."

Julie hugs me tightly. I'm startled at first. No one has touched me in so long that it's like I don't remember how to let myself be embraced. Her hug feels *unnatural*, but Julie persists, ignoring my vibes. I can tell she's determined to break down the barrier between us and bring me back from wherever it is that I've gone. She moves closer and rests her head on my shoulder. "I don't get it either, Bean, but I'm here for you. And this time I'm not leaving."

"I'm a mess. I know I am. But I don't know how to move forward because Sam's death still doesn't make sense on any level. Maybe it shouldn't matter, because he's gone and he's obviously not coming back; but to me, it matters. If he took his own life, then I never really knew him. He was a stranger, or worse yet, he was a fraud, and how am I supposed to mourn someone like that?"

Julie nods. "I get that. I really do."

This is the first time I've articulated my confusion out loud, and as my words sink in, I feel even more hopeless because I can't see any way out of my dilemma. I slide down and rest my head in Julie's lap and lie there thinking. Suddenly, an idea comes to me. I sit up and turn to face Julie so I can gauge her reaction. "This might sound totally crazy, but what would you think about trying to figure out exactly what happened that night?"

Julie doesn't say anything for a while. I can see her mind turning this idea over. "You know, Bean, we never talked about it."

"About what?" I ask.

"What we think happened. I mean, I was here. I saw him, and I know how it looked, but it makes no sense to me, either. It didn't then, and it doesn't now. But whenever I try to defend Sam by telling people it wasn't a suicide, they think I'm crazy, and I kinda get that. But you and I never once talked about it."

I nod. "I know. I guess I was afraid to. As sure as I am that it wasn't a suicide, I can't come up with any other reasonable explanation. Can you?"

"Not really, but I'd be willing to try to figure this out with you, Bean. If that's what you want. If you're serious, I mean."

"How, though? It's been so long, where would we even begin?" I ask.

"Well, you told me that the cops and detectives did a shitty job, that they never really considered any other possibilities. And while we both know how incriminating it looked, it's at least worth considering other scenarios. I mean someone could have snuck in, strangled him, and then made it look like a suicide."

"But we didn't see anyone, and we were both here all night."

"Yeah, but it was totally chaotic. Your parents and their friends were so loud we had to shut the den door just to hear our movie. Remember? And I get that it's not a very *likely* scenario, but it's at least *possible*. Think about all the crime shows we've watched over the years, with all those twists and turns. I'm just saying, crazy shit can happen, and the answers aren't always the most obvious ones."

I nod slowly as I think this over.

"Did the cops or detectives ask about Sam's mental state? Did they get that he wasn't depressed, that he didn't have a messed-up family life or a shitty social life, and that he wasn't on any heavy drugs? I mean he was basically a happy dude with tons of friends and a nice girlfriend, and I don't see how someone like that could suddenly snap and decide to end his life, no matter how angry and upset he might have been at the time. There has to be more to it."

"He and Jenny had recently broken up. At least I think they did, because I didn't see her at all those last few weeks. But, yes," I say, nodding, "I explained the rest to them, but they didn't listen. I'm sure they wrote me off as the crazy little sister who was afraid to admit that her brother was massively messed up. Plus, I'm pretty sure they wanted to wrap up the investigation as quickly as possible and get the hell out of our way."

"That's what I figured," Julie says. "And that's exactly why we should dig deeper."

"But what if we're both wrong, and he really did it?" I ask. "What then?"

Julie shrugs. "It can't be any worse than it is now, right? I honestly think we owe it to Sam to at least *try* to find out what happened. Can you imagine if everyone thought you took your life and you hadn't? How shitty would that be?"

"It's not shitty for Sam. He's gone. It's my family that has to go around feeling wrecked."

"Right, that's what I meant. It's totally messed up all around."

"You know what I really want?" I ask.

"What?"

"I want this to be *someone's* fault, just not anyone in my family."

"I get that," Julie says.

"If we decide we're going to go through with this, what *exactly* are you thinking we'd do?"

"Statistically speaking, most people who are murdered knew their assailant, which also makes sense because there was no sign of forced entry and nothing was stolen. I guess we'd start by talking to everyone Sam might have spoken to his last day to find out if there's anything we don't already know."

"Ugh," I say, thinking immediately about Skip, the one person who might know something or have some insight about what happened, but who's mysteriously MIA. I feel queasy, though I'm not exactly sure why.

"Bean?"

I look up. Tears start falling down my cheeks. I quickly wipe them away, but I'm not quick enough that Julie doesn't notice.

She wraps her arms around me. "Bean, what's wrong?"

I shrug.

"Please tell me. You know I won't judge you."

I sit with the feeling a bit longer before blurting out, "I feel guilty."

"What? Why do *you* feel guilty? You had nothing to do with it. We were in another room when it happened. What are you even talking about?"

"The accident. It was my fault. The roads were horrible. Why did I make Sam drive me? And on top of that, I *knew* something was going to happen, but I didn't listen to myself."

Julie frowns. "What do you mean, you *knew*?"

"I told you I felt horribly uneasy that entire day, but I didn't really try to figure out why."

"I remember you telling me that you felt off, but you have to know that having a premonition and being able to alter the future are two entirely different things. But wait, are you saying you believe there's a connection between our accident and his death?"

I shrug. "I don't know for sure, but it's possible."

"If that's the case, then I'm just as guilty as you. How many times did I text you to see if someone could come get me? I could've walked over. My parents would never have known. Or why didn't I simply suggest we skip our sleepover? I wanted to talk to you about something, but it wasn't urgent. It could have waited, and spying on Skip's party was clearly never going to happen in that storm, and that was our only *big* plan for the night. So, I'm just as much to blame as you are, if not more. But the thing is, we don't know for sure if these two things are connected, so I don't think we should beat ourselves up over it."

I nod. "You're right. Even for Sam it seems like a very big leap."

"That's why this idea of yours is solid. Even if we can't find out exactly how it all went down, maybe we can at least learn enough to allow you to let go of your guilt."

I nod. "That would be nice."

"Why don't you go shower. I'll make you some breakfast, feed Dawg, and start dealing with the laundry," Julie says. "If I help, maybe we can find a few hours to hang out."

We slide off the bed, and she hugs me again. There's something so intense and primal about our connection that for the first time in months I feel grounded, like maybe I do have a reason to stay on the planet. It also feels great to have someone else taking charge.

"I'm so sorry for pushing you away," I say.

"It's okay. We're back now, and that's all that matters."

I grab her hand and squeeze. "BFFs?"

"Always and forever," Julie says, which is how we have always said goodbye to each other. But hearing this now, I realize that Julie can't guarantee she'll be with me forever any more than Sam could. It seems the only thing that's really *forever* is death.

I stand under the water for what feels like hours as a million thoughts swirl around my head. For months I've been feeling lost, lonely, and unsure of who I am. Before all this mess with Sam happened and things got cloudy, I knew exactly who I was. For seventh-grade English we had to write a short descriptive paragraph about ourselves in the third person. I wrote this:

Bean is a nature girl, drawn to earth and heaven and everything in between. She's spiritual and inquisitive, always a seeker of deeper truths. Her brown mane hangs nearly to her waist, and her eyes, which many say are her most striking feature, are sea-foam green. Her family includes three brothers, one of whom is her forever soul mate. Bean enjoys reading, writing, breathing, and believing.

Asked to write the same paragraph today, I'd write:

Bean is a girl with a dead brother . . . who may have chosen to end his life.

I let that sit for a second but then realize that's not really the end of the story. It's not nearly that simple. We've been left with so many unanswered questions that I can only imagine that every member of my family is, to some degree, carrying around their own suffocating guilt. We don't dare talk about it, but I'm sure we're all wondering the same thing: How could we live with Sam for seventeen years and not see that blackness pervaded his soul? How could he possibly have fooled us all into believing he was healthy and happy if he wasn't? Or, if he was murdered, who did it and why?

FOUR

"Close your eyes," Julie instructs as I walk into the kitchen. I do as I'm told. "Okay, open them."

Julie's standing in front of me holding a plate with two perfectly toasted Eggo waffles, melted butter and syrup running down the sides, and a single red-striped candle burning atop a clump of whipped cream. "Happy birthday, Bean! It isn't much, but it's the best I could manage given your pathetic fridge sitch."

I laugh. "Trust me, this day is already way better than I expected, thanks to you. As for food, well, it's pretty bleak. Ever since the neighborhood food train ended, we've been exclusively eating take-out, and rarely do we eat together. The last meal we ate as a family was on Christmas Eve, and I told you how bad that was."

I imagine post-loss holidays are difficult for all families. The rituals you never pay much attention to feel especially painful when one of your family members is no longer with you, playing their role. We'd just survived the funeral, the departure of out-of-town friends and relatives, and the ridiculous amount of uneaten and unappetizing food being left for us daily by well-meaning neighbors, when Thanksgiving hit.

I have no idea if anyone asked us to join them for Thanksgiving dinner, but I wouldn't blame them if they hadn't. After all, why would anyone intentionally invite sadness into their home on such a festive occasion? When Dad asked us to put on our coats that chilly Thanksgiving evening, we did as we were told, no questions asked. I assumed we were going somewhere for dinner, because it was already past six and there was definitely no meal being prepared in our kitchen. Though Mom wasn't as bad off as she is now, she had by then already surrendered most of her kitchen duties. Even still, I was shocked and horrified when Dad turned into the parking lot of the Lakeview Diner, a run-down truck stop on the outskirts of town, the sort of place you went if you had absolutely *no* other options. It was sad. No, it was completely pathetic.

The ugly, cold, corrugated-steel diner stood by itself on a lonely stretch of highway, and despite its name, it had no lake view, unless you counted the slushy puddles scattered throughout the potholed parking lot. Dad parked, shut off the engine, then exited and walked over to help Mom out of the front passenger seat. My brothers and I exchanged looks in the backseat. When they were both clear of the car, Adam whispered, "Well, this is a new low, even for us." We got out of the car and followed behind them, marching single file up the stairs with our heads down, though it was doubtful we'd see anyone we knew there.

Without waiting for assistance from the hostess, as the sign directed, we settled into the closest available grey-and-red-striped Naugahyde booth. There were very few other diners, just a couple of truck drivers and some senior citizens, but it felt like they were all deliberately averting their eyes. I don't know if they somehow knew about Sam or if they simply couldn't imagine why a family would be spending their Thanksgiving at a diner. What they didn't know was that we were no longer a *whole* family.

The meal was bland and mushy. If I'd been blindfolded, I couldn't have told you where on my plate the mashed potatoes left off and the peas began. Worse yet, it was served on paper plates with plastic silverware, because, the waitress explained, their dishwasher was on the fritz. We ate in silence except for a few "Please pass the . . ." We were like those people you sometimes see at a restaurant who look like they have absolutely nothing to say to one another, and you wonder why they bother staying together. In our case, it was blood and grief.

I kept trying to think of something we could discuss that would take our minds off our current predicament, but nothing came to mind. What was there to say? Dad's main objective must have been to stay away from our house for as long as possible; he never eats dessert, yet he ordered a slice of lemon merengue pie with coffee and then asked for two refills. I wanted to get out of there so badly I started tapping my fork against the table, a nervous habit of mine, which annoys the hell out of Dad. But that night he didn't say a word. He sipped his coffee and stared off into space, presumably lost in thoughts that were likely better not shared. All I really wanted was to put the day behind us. For better or worse, we'd survived our first holiday without Sam, and that felt like a monumental accomplishment in and of itself.

But Christmas is a way bigger deal, because it's not about a single meal or even a single day. Beginning December 1, the dads in our neighborhood would begin going to extreme lengths to outdo each other with their outdoor holiday displays. Our dad, engineer extraordinaire, had always been one of the most competitive. But this year our outdoor decorations never made it out of the basement. Looking back, I wish we'd made the effort just so we wouldn't have stuck out so badly, but none of us had that foresight.

Inside the house, it was no different. Maybe we believed the holiday would go by faster if we ignored it. But that didn't feel right either. Then, on December 23, Dad arrived home from work with a sorry-ass tree tied to the top of his car, and by the next afternoon it had been decorated—by whom I don't know—with hideous red glass balls and cheesy silver icicles. Every time I walked by, I felt sorry for it, because it looked so gaudy and garish. Worse even than how flashy it was were how few presents were underneath—just five, which all had been sent from distant relatives who normally wouldn't have gotten us anything.

In previous years, we'd piled into our ancient Volvo station wagon and headed into the woods in mid-December. We'd cut down a tree that Sam chose after conferring with the tree's spirit. Years ago, he'd convinced us that trees, like people, have souls, and that having a tree in your home that hadn't given its permission to be felled could have serious consequences. Once home, we'd decorate it. First, we'd hang lights, then strings of popcorn and cranberry, then our homemade ornaments and fresh-baked gingerbread men. Finally, we'd top it with a big silver star. All the while we'd be drinking hot chocolate or eggnog and listening to cheesy Christmas CDs featuring Frank Sinatra, Bing Crosby, Andy Williams, or my favorite, the Chipmunks.

None of that happened this year. December was a horribly long, morose month. However, on Christmas Eve morning, Dad announced that we'd be attending midnight services, as had been our custom. Normally, Mom would have prepared a prime rib dinner with all the fixings and a veggie meatloaf for me, but this year we ate frozen TV dinners on foldout snack trays in our den while watching old Christmas movies to stay awake. About an hour before we were to leave, Mom asked me to help her make the gingerbread men cookies. I thought this was a good sign, as she hadn't done anything slightly Christmassy all season, and she hadn't baked once since Sam left, even though it was something she'd loved to do. Little did I know that those seemingly innocent cookies would turn a bad Christmas into a nightmarish one.

Before heading out, she and I quickly hung the cookies on

the tree, which made us a bit late. This seemed a good thing, though, because by the time we arrived, the sanctuary was lit only by candles, and we were able to sneak unnoticed into the space behind the last pew. It was our first time back since Sam's funeral, and I was worried our presence might cause a scene. When the service ended, however, my parents, especially Mom, were swarmed with people offering hugs and tears and asking insensitive questions: "How long had Sam been feeling blue?" "Had he made previous attempts to take his life?" "Was he seeing someone for his depression?"

I'm sure they hadn't meant any harm, but it hurt just the same, and doubly so for Mom, who I could tell was interpreting every remark as an attack on her for being an unfit, negligent mother. I'd been asked similar questions at school, but Mom had been pretty much sequestered inside our house, and she probably hadn't heard these types of accusations before. Her eyes began to tear and before long she was sobbing uncontrollably. After what seemed like an eternity, but was probably only ten minutes, Dad managed to get her into our car. As we drove off, I reached up from the backseat to rub her back, but I could tell she was too far gone to be comforted by my touch.

Dad stopped the car at the walkway to our front door, and Mom and I got out. He knew she wanted to be back in bed, alone with her thoughts, and this was the quickest route. I held her elbow and guided her up the walk and inside the front door. When I turned on the living room lights, Mom pointed to the

Christmas tree and hysterically cried, "For Christ's sake, who would have done such a cruel thing?" On the tree hung twenty-four heads of decapitated gingerbread men, their bodies strewn beneath them on the tree skirt. It looked like a scene from a horror movie, and was doubly horrific given the circumstances of Sam's death. Dad heard Mom's screams and came running in from the garage. He hugged her to him while trying to shield her face. Together we guided her back to their room, which is where she's pretty much been holed up ever since. Dad and I eventually figured out what had happened: We hadn't let the cookies harden sufficiently, so they'd broken at their weakest spot. It was some consolation, but not much.

I wish now that we'd gone away for Christmas. In the end, it's the unfamiliarity of the familiar that gets you. In most families, it's probably the youngest children who are most excited about the Christmas holidays. But in our family, it was Sam who brought the holidays to life. He loved everything about it, from picking out the tree, to choosing the best branch for each ornament, to personally making us each a unique gift, which we all chose to open last, because they were *that* special.

I tried to convince myself that if we could survive that first holiday season without Sam, things would slowly start to improve. But that didn't happen, and now I wonder if it ever will. No matter how many years go by, I know Thanksgiving and Christmas will always remind us of Sam. I suppose it must be that way for all families who experience deaths around holidays.

From then forward, your holidays become not the "holiest" but the "hollowest" days of the year.

But the holidays are now long gone, and I'm desperate to put these memories behind me. Julie's here, it's my birthday, and I want to try to turn my frown upside down, so I make a wish and blow out my birthday candle.

As I eat my Eggos, my eyes are drawn to the framed poster hanging over the small desk in the corner of our kitchen. It had been a gift to my mother from her best friend. It depicted a duck floating on a pond. Underneath was written "A good hostess is like a duck, calm and serene on the surface, yet paddling like hell underneath." The top of the poster was inscribed with the words "To Peggy, the Consummate Hostess, with love, much admiration (and a tad bit of jealousy), Letty.

Not anymore. That woman who'd once been the envy of her friends—efficiently and gracefully running a house with four kids, a husband, and a dog, forever attending to the needs of friends and neighbors, and usually entertaining weekly—has all but evaporated into thin air, and I have no idea how to get her to rematerialize, or if it's even possible.

Julie follows my gaze. "How's she doing? Any better?"

"Not really."

"Wow, I'm sorry. Is she getting help? Going to therapy or taking anything?"

"Dr. Marks stops by every once in a while, and she's been to a therapist a few times and he's prescribed stuff, though I have no idea what. But whatever it is, it doesn't seem to be working. She still spends ninety percent of her time in their bedroom. I know I'm bad, but she's like a whole other degree of badness."

"That sucks."

I nod. "What can I say? It is what it is."

"I put a load of dirty laundry from the hall hamper into the washing machine," Julie says. "And I ironed your dad's shirts that were on the ironing board. I also fed Dawg, but she didn't eat much." She points to the mostly full dog bowl sitting next to the back door.

"Wow, you got a shit-ton done. How long was I in the shower?"

She nods. "A while, but I'm good. Just happy to be hanging with you."

I smile. "Me too." I point to my empty plate. "And those were really good." I push my seat back from the table and stand up. "I'm going to make Mom some breakfast and quickly clean her bathroom. When I'm done, I can probably hang out for an hour or so."

Breakfast tray in hand, I knock on my parents' door and hear a faint sound. Mom's voice, like the rest of her, has shrunk. I open the door and involuntarily gasp. It shouldn't be such a shock—after all, she didn't deteriorate overnight—and yet, whenever I see her, I still find it horribly unsettling. Mom used to be very pretty, for a mom anyway. She had a flawless complexion, and she was always super-stylish, even if she was just walking to the mailbox. We aren't rich, so she never had the latest fashions, but you wouldn't know that from the outfits she managed to put together, mostly from thrift store finds. Plus, she was in great shape thanks to her Dancercise and Pilates classes. Now she looks downright ghostlike. She's probably lost twenty pounds, maybe more, her hair is a matted mess, and the circles under her eyes are getting larger and darker by the day. She's wearing one of Sam's oversize T-shirts with an illustrated wolf and a word bubble: "Little Red Riding Hood lied. I never laid a paw on her." I can't help but wonder if it's possible to die from grief, because that seems to be the direction she's headed.

"I brought you some breakfast, and while I'm here I'm going to tidy up your bathroom."

"Thanks," she says, "but you don't have to bother with the bathroom." I want to scream, "Really? Then who the hell will clean it?" But I bite my tongue. What would be the point of calling her out?

"I don't mind," I say. "Just please try to eat something. You're wasting away."

I head to the bathroom to start cleaning. As I'm leaning over the tub with a scrub brush, my shoelace gets caught on a handle of a small drawer on the bottom of an antique trunk that Mom uses as a table for her soaps and bath salts. I never even knew this drawer existed. After unhooking my lace, I glance in the drawer and discover dozens of pill bottles. I pull one out and then another. They're all *full*. Shit. This can't be good. I toss them all into a small clear trash bag and storm back into the bedroom.

"What's up with this?" I say, holding out the bag.

I've definitely startled her. She sighs and stares at me for a second. "I know it's wrong, but I didn't know what else to do. Your father is absolutely convinced I'm depressed and anxiety ridden, and he believes those pills will somehow *fix* me. But they won't." She shakes her head defiantly. "I know they won't, and even if they could, that's not how I want to heal. I have to work through this in my own way. Rather than creating a scene with your father, which I'm not up for, I've let him think I'm taking everything I've been prescribed."

"That's really wrong on so many levels. First of all, you aren't okay. Maybe you are depressed and maybe," I joggle the pill bottles, "these would help."

She pats the bed. "Bean, please come sit beside me. Let's talk for a minute." She moves over and I sit next to her, but remain rigid, and I raise my eyebrows to let her know I'm serious. "I took them for the first couple of months," she says. "I really did. But they made me feel numb, and I don't want to feel numb. Besides, I'm not depressed. I've read all about it, and it doesn't resonate with me. I'm sure it looks like I'm wallowing in self-pity, but I'm trying to process all this in a way that feels right for me." She pushes her bangs out of her face and then lowers her voice as if confessing. "Perhaps the hardest part for me is that I didn't receive any sign that this was coming. Did you?"

Mom strongly believes in signs. For every important life event, she's received a sign that told her what was about to happen.

I can understand that having no warning about something as tragic as this would throw her.

"I did," I say, happy to be having a real conversation with her for a change. "I knew something wasn't right from the minute I woke up that day, but I couldn't figure out what it was."

"Well, I didn't feel anything, which doesn't make sense. Why give someone a sixth sense and then turn it off when it's most needed?"

"Maybe it was for the best. How could you really have prepared yourself?" I ask.

She nods, as if this is something she hasn't considered.

"But back to these," I say, once again shaking the pill bottles. "It's really scary that you have all these stored up."

"I promise I wasn't *storing* them for any purpose. I just didn't know what to do with them. And I read somewhere that for the sake of the environment, you shouldn't flush them down the toilet."

"Okay, but I'm sure they're expensive, and on top of that, you've been lying to Dad and your psychiatrist. That's not right. You have to come clean with them," I say, looking her in the eyes. "There's no way I can keep this secret for you. It's too big."

She nods. "You're right, it wouldn't be fair of me to ask you to do that. And speaking of fair, I just want to say I'm really, really sorry for being such a crappy mom. All these months I've wanted to reach out and share things with you—I really have, but it's hard because the three of us were so intrinsically linked and—"

I put my hand out to stop her from saying anything more. "It's okay, Mom. I know what you're going to say." I'm on the verge of tears, but I don't want her to notice. I need her to believe I'm okay and therefore she should be okay. But it's all a big fat lie, and I'm sure she senses that.

Before we lost Sam, I considered our family fairly close. We basically got along pretty well; we didn't raise our voices to one another very often, and we had family dinners at least four times a week. But since Sam passed, I realize that our closeness was actually fake, or maybe *superficial* is a more accurate description. In actuality, we were deeply divided. Dad, Adam, and Chase don't believe in anything they can't see with their own eyes. They go to church if Mom asks, but I'm pretty sure they don't believe in God or any other higher power. They move through life and deal with obstacles without question, introspection, or a search for deeper meaning. Sam's death, as horrible as it was, is something they all seem to have accepted and moved on from. As someone remarked at the funeral, "They're solid as rocks," as if being a cold, hard inanimate object was actually something to be admired.

Mom and I—and Sam when he was alive—believe that the world is governed by myriad magical and mystical energies and forces, and that obstacles are presented to us in order for our souls to grow. We could see and feel that a higher power was at work around us at all times. And this all made complete sense— until Sam passed. But now, try as I might, I can't see how my soul, or his, will grow from this experience.

Mom senses that I'm lost in thought, and she attempts to

bring me back. "Bean, sweetie, can you be patient with me for just a bit longer? And can we please keep this," she says, grabbing my hand with the pills, "between us for the time being?"

I cross my arms and frown. "I don't know. How long are we talking?" I don't appreciate the position she's putting me in. Everything she's said sounds somewhat sane, but what do I know about mental health and depression? Plus, I seriously don't need to be dealing with her shit on top of my own.

"I wish I could give you a time frame, but I really can't. I'm spending a lot of time meditating and doing deep breathing work, and I really believe I'm beginning to see the light at the end of the tunnel. I know I'm going to come out of this fog soon, I just need a bit more time." She pauses. "How about this? You take the pills and dispose of them in whatever way is best, and I promise that if I feel myself slipping, I'll let you know and at that point I'll come clean with your father, or I'll let you."

"No. I can't trust you to be the judge of yourself. I'm giving you two weeks max, and then either you tell Dad, or I will."

Her eyes widen. "That's not much time, but I understand your concerns. Just don't do anything rash, and promise me you'll let me know before you say anything to him."

I nod. We hug for the first time in months, but rather than feeling loving support, I feel more like a coconspirator. I rise from the bed and notice the overflowing basket of unopened condolence letters and cards on the shelf below her nightstand. "It doesn't look like you've made much of a dent in those," I say, pointing. I'd read the first twenty or so that arrived but stopped when I realized they were all addressed to my parents, as if my brothers and I hadn't also suffered a loss. "Do you want me to get them out of here? Put them away somewhere till you're ready to read them?"

She nods. "That's a good idea. And was that Julie's voice I heard earlier?"

I nod.

"It's been a while since she's been around, hasn't it?"

"Yeah. That's my fault. Anyway, she showed up today to wish me a happy birthday." I wasn't planning on mentioning this, but suddenly I feel emboldened to speak my mind and let her know that Sam wasn't her only child, that I'm here and I still need mothering.

"Oh, Bean, come here," she says, motioning me to her.

I walk back over, she sits up and opens her arms, and I fall into them. Even though she's bony and weak, I have to admit that it feels good to have someone in the family acknowledge my birthday.

"I'm so sorry," she says. "How could I forget? It seems I've lost all track of time. One day flows into the next. I barely know what month it is, let alone the day of the week. I'm so very, very sorry, and I promise I'll make it up to you. You truly deserve better. What mother forgets her own child's birthday?" She starts to tear up, and I can't help but feel horrid for bringing up my stupid birthday.

"It's okay, Mom. And if it makes you feel any better, no one else in the family remembered either. I guess we've all got more important things on our minds."

"Yes, but that's no excuse."

"We'll celebrate when we're all in a better place," I say. "I'll be fifteen all year long."

"That's a deal. And thanks for being so understanding. I hope to be back on my feet soon. I miss being a mom. I miss all of it."

I kiss her on the forehead. "I miss you, too," I say, which is the understatement of the century. In the hallway, I consider tossing out the cards, because it's hard to imagine that there'll ever be a day when she'll be interested in reading them, but I decide it's not my call, so I place them on the tip-top shelf of the hall closet, where it's unlikely Mom will see them.

When I walk back into the kitchen, Julie asks how it went, and I tell her.

"Any idea how you're supposed to properly dispose of meds?" I say, holding up the bag.

Julie nods. "I'll take them. There's a collection box at my grandma's nursing home, and we're having dinner with her tonight."

"You promise you won't let anyone see you do it?"

"Promise. It won't be a problem," she says.

A few minutes later we put on our coats, hats, and mittens and head out the backyard, down toward the lake. The sun is still shining and it is beautiful outside, but it doesn't feel like it's

quite made it over the freezing mark. It's been a brutal winter—
in more ways than one.

Julie stops abruptly when we reach the barrier I've built on the
ice around the doe. "I haven't asked, but I'm curious," she says.
"What's up with this?"

I shrug. "I don't know, really. I just thought it was strange
that she ended up here, right beside our dock, the morning
after Sam died."

"Do you think she's somehow connected to him?"

"I'm probably wrong, but I think it's possible that she *is* the
deer we hit that night."

Julie looks a bit confused or maybe concerned. "But we killed
it, remember? It was lying motionless in the road."

"Yeah, I know, but what if it wasn't dead? Remember when
my dad went out to inspect the damage to his car? He didn't see
a deer. Maybe she was only injured and in shock, and after we
went into the house, she recovered, sort of, and then got up, but
made it only as far as the lake before she collapsed."

Julie thinks this over for a few long seconds. She shrugs. "Sounds
pretty far-fetched to me," she says, and then right before I'm about
to take the idea back, because somehow saying it out loud sounds
more ridiculous than I'd imagined, she adds, "but I suppose it's
possible. It didn't make sense that your dad didn't see it."

"I know, and I feel like ever since then, he doesn't totally trust
me. He thinks I'm hiding something from him, that there's more
to our accident than I'm letting on."

"We could prove it to him if we could look below the ice to see if she has a gash on her belly."

Relief falls over me. I fear that I've been creating my own reality, that living in a bubble these last few months has caused me to have totally delusional thoughts. Of course, it's also possible that she's humoring me because she senses how fragile I am and how tentative our reunion feels, and she doesn't want to do or say anything that will jeopardize our friendship and send me back into hiding.

"Right," I say, "if only the ice wasn't still so thick." For a second, I consider saying nothing else, but I decide that if we are back to being BFFs, then I've got to be honest with her. "If it is the same doe, that would mean that Sam's blood is mixed with hers, which would totally explain why I've felt so oddly protective of her, because she's my last link to Sam. Even Dawg had a strange reaction to her; the first time she saw the doe, she started licking her face." I hold my breath, waiting for Julie's reaction.

She hardly hesitates. "Okay, I get it, sort of, but I have to tell you that everyone else thinks you've kind of lost your mind."

I feel like I've been slapped hard across the face. I've been living in my own messed-up, isolated world for so long that I haven't stopped to think about what anyone might be thinking or saying about me. "Why? What're they saying?" I ask, but I'm afraid to hear the answer.

"That you're like a zombie. You walk around with that hoodie pulled over your head, and you don't talk to anyone. And no one can make any sense of this barrier you've built, or why you spend so much time out here on the ice alone with this dead deer. Kids are starting to compare you to Sam."

I jerk my head up. "What are you talking about?"

"No one would have thought much about it if Sam did something like this." She points to the barrier. "But it seems out of character for you, so everyone's a bit freaked out."

"Freaked out about what? They think I'm going to kill myself like they think Sam did?" I say, sounding as angry and defensive as I feel. How will I ever be able to face anyone again knowing that they not only think I'm crazy, but also suicidal?

Julie puts her arm around my shoulder. "Bean, please don't take this the wrong way. Everyone's worried because they care about you."

"Do *you* think Sam was out there? Do *you* think that's why he's dead?"

Julie vigorously shakes her head. "No, you know I loved Sam."

I move away and let Julie's arm fall off my shoulder. "You're not answering my question," I say.

"Okay, honestly, I'd be lying if I said I haven't wondered if his Inuit beliefs might have had something to do with his death. I don't know exactly how or why, but it's crossed my mind. Hasn't it crossed yours?"

I suddenly feel enraged. How could Julie think that the Inuit—who, according to Sam, are the most peaceful and resilient people on the planet—could have had anything to do with his death? She really knew him, yet it sounds like she believes Sam was crazy or deranged or unhinged, just like everyone else does. My heart is beating a mile a minute. I want to scream, but it's probably best if I breathe deeply and try to chill out. "Let's walk to the Enchanted Forest Island. I need to think."

We hardly say a word during the ten or so minutes it takes for us to trek across the snow-covered ice to the island, and I can't help wondering what she's thinking. Does she wish she never came over today? Does she think I'm too crazy to be friends with now? Have things changed so much between us that we'll never be able to be besties again? Does she think I'm a freak? Do I scare her? Shit, I don't know what to think. Losing Sam was one thing. Then I lost Mom. And now, am I losing Julie . . . *again*?

The Enchanted Forest Island encompasses about eight or so acres. It's dense with old-growth red pine and other deciduous trees, and in the spring the ground is thickly carpeted with violets and lilies of the valley. It's a magical spot, and it was one of Sam's favorite places. He claimed it when he was around nine, and over the years he designed a series of walking paths and three fire pits. Next to one of the pits he built a lean-to, where he camped out on many nights, no matter the season. We make our way along one of the paths I luckily know by heart, because it's currently buried in a foot or more of snow. Suddenly, something black darts between the trees about fifty yards ahead.

"Did you see that?" I ask, pointing.

"No, what was it?"

"I think it was a wolf. I've been seeing a big black one around this island ever since Sam passed. The first time I saw it was the day after Sam's death, when I found the doe on the ice. There were large paw prints that circled the doe, and when I looked up, I saw it standing on the shore of the island looking at me. And since then I've had a few short glimpses of it, always on or around this island. Seems strange that it would live alone and stay here, because there can't be much wildlife to support it. But I keep thinking that maybe it's important because it showed up when Sam passed, and wolves were his major totem animal."

"You've seen a wolf in broad daylight more than once?" Julie says.

I nod.

"And it had circled the doe, but hadn't eaten it?"

"I know it sounds crazy."

"What if it has rabies?" Julie asks.

"It's really big and healthy. There's no chance it's sick."

"Has anyone else seen it?"

I can't help but wonder if she thinks I'm making this up or, worse yet, imagining things.

"Wait. Do you think it's *Sam*?"

I shrug and smile, feeling relieved that, at the very least, she's willing to humor me. "It's a lot to hope for, but if he were to come back, I bet he'd choose to reincarnate as a wolf."

Julie smiles. "Definitely! Let me know if you see it again. I'd love to get a look at it."

About ten minutes later, we arrive at the closest fire pit. I use my mittens to clear off a spot for us on a log, and we both sit down. The fragrant scent of pine is heavenly. I've always thought that it smelled better here than anywhere else. I was worried that I wouldn't be able to handle coming here due to the island's connection to Sam, but I'm relieved to learn that being here feels somehow very *right*. I feel him more strongly than I've felt him anywhere else. I close my eyes and take a few very long, deep breaths. I'm happy to be here and elated to have Julie sitting next to me.

I decide to be honest with her to the extent that I'm ready to be. If what I say scares her, I'm no worse off than I was before. "I'd like to talk about something you said earlier. I'd be lying if I told you that the thought of Sam's death being in some way connected to his Inuit beliefs hasn't crossed my mind. But I really doubt it. I bet the Inuit wouldn't even consider taking their own lives. It seems out of character from what Sam told me about them."

Julie nods. "You're probably right. But after we collided with the deer, he seemed so horrified, or shocked, or something. I'd never seen him like that. I wondered later if maybe he'd crossed some Inuit line that he couldn't come back from."

"I don't know everything about the Inuit, but I don't think so. Whenever he caught a fish or ran over a squirrel or rabbit accidently, he gave the animal a bit of water and mingled a little of his blood with theirs. It was how he made peace with their souls.

I don't know why a deer would be any different, and it wasn't like he killed it on purpose."

"You're right. And creatures seem to totally understand the respect he had for them. I still remember the first time I slept in the lean-to with you guys. I'd never experienced anything like that."

I laugh. "There was that mouse that wouldn't leave us alone and a squirrel who kept climbing all over him."

"And then in the morning, a rabbit hopped right in front of us with her babies following behind her. Things like that never seemed to happen unless Sam was around. It was like his presence or energy made animals totally chill out."

"That's a good way of putting it."

"I'm curious, what did Skip think of all the Inuit stuff?"

I shrug. "They were both into nature, so I think he went along with it because of Sam."

"Cool that they found each other. Everyone needs a best bud," Julie says, smiling at me. "I've also been wondering if anyone ever bullied Sam?"

"He definitely got into his share of fights over the years, mostly in elementary and middle school, and I'm guessing they all had something to do with his Inuit beliefs, his long hair, or the bandanas he always wore. But I don't think it was anything serious, and by the end of middle school, everyone had pretty much accepted him for who he was. Why?"

Julie looks like she's afraid to answer my question. "Sometimes there are things going on that no one has any idea about, like with that sixteen-year-old boy in Silver Bay who hung himself supposedly because he was mortified that some kid posted a video of him jerking off. I think sometimes guys' hormones, or maybe that coupled with drugs, drive them to make really stupid choices. I wonder if it's possible that something was going on in his life that in the moment seemed overwhelming to him."

"No way. And if there was anything like that going on, he definitely would've told me, and this town is so small that if there were some video floating around out there, we'd have heard about it." I sound confident, but I'm not. As much as I'd love to believe there were no secrets between us, I assume there were *plenty* of things I didn't know about Sam. "Do you think there's any possibility he might have done it on a dare?"

"Who the hell would hang themselves on a dare? He could be wild, but he wasn't crazy."

"I'm sorry. I'm not trying to upset you, but I think if we're really going to try to figure this out, we have to consider every possible scenario. I definitely don't think he was crazy, but he did some pretty extreme things from time to time. It seemed like he'd try anything at least once."

"Taking my dad's car without asking, jumping off the house into a leaf pile, rappelling down the side of some crazy-steep cliff, hitchhiking all over the state—those things he'd do. But killing himself? Seriously? Like you said, he wasn't psycho or depressed, and he didn't believe he was immortal. He broke way too many bones for that to be the case. Are *you* starting to believe he might have chosen to take his own life?"

Julie shrugs. "I'm getting every last thought out of my head. I want to be completely honest with you about everything I'm thinking. I hope you're not mad at me for suggesting—"

"I'm not," I say, but I am. Julie is questioning Sam's sanity just like everyone else. I thought we were back together, a united team, but now I realize I'm still all alone on my own island. "I'm getting cold," I say. "Ready to head back?"

We walk back along the same path, which is much easier to follow now that we've packed down the snow. "Do you remember that before our sleepover," Julie says, "on the night Sam died, I told you that I was going to share really big news with you?"

"Yeah, I completely forgot about that. What was it?"

"Richie Branson asked me about you. He said he wanted to take you out, and he asked me to find out if you'd be down with that."

I stop dead in my tracks. "Seriously?"

She nods.

I start stamping my feet. "Fuck! Why didn't you say something earlier?" Of course, I know exactly why she didn't. It wasn't exactly a normal night, and there hasn't been a normal one since. "I can't imagine what he thinks of me now. I've totally blown it, haven't I?"

Julie grins from ear to ear.

I jump up and down and then stop and stare at her with my hands on my hips. "Spill. What do you know?"

"He asked about you again last Friday. He wanted to know how you were doing. He's worried about you, but I also got the feeling that he's still into you."

"I find that really hard to believe. Practically every girl in our school has a crush on him. Why would he choose me, 'the zombie girl' he doesn't even know? Plus, isn't he too old? I mean I've never even had a boyfriend my own age, let alone one that's two years older."

"He doesn't care about all those girls who are always chasing after him. And I know he doesn't know you, but he definitely wants to."

"How do you know that? How do you even know him?"

"I got moved up to advanced physics, and he's my lab partner. He's so good-looking that you assume he'll be stuck up. But he's not. If anything, he's painfully shy. I think all the attention he gets really freaks him out. He actually said that girls come on too strongly, and he doesn't like it. What high school guy on the planet has ever said that?"

This Richie news stirs something inside of me; it's like a part of me that had been shut down has suddenly been turned back on, which feels good and then not so good. I feel guiltier than I did before. Like it isn't okay for me to have a future if Sam can't have one. Like somehow moving forward will put even more distance between Sam and me. But I know this is insane and I have to stop it. Sam would have wanted me to have a life. I know he would have.

On the way back to my house, we talk about Richie and what Julie should say to him. When we get inside, Julie says she should get home to study for a history test. "Happy birthday, Bean. I know this wasn't the best birthday you've ever had, but I hope it's the beginning of better times."

I hug her. "I'm so grateful you came and knocked some sense into me. I was an idiot to push you away. And thanks for the beautiful journal. I'm sure I'll have it filled up in no time."

She smiles and hugs me back. "The only thing I care about is that the BFFs are reunited."

"Always and forever," I say.

After Julie leaves, I go back to my room, sit on my bed, and as soon as I do, all the doubts I've ever had start stacking up in my head. Why did Sam and Jenny break up? Where the hell did Skip go? Was Sam being bullied? Blackmailed? Dared? Could he have taken some drug that made him go crazy? The autopsy showed no drugs in his system, but is it possible they missed something or that there are drugs that are undetectable? Do Inuit believe killing a deer is an unforgiveable sin? Do deer even exist in the Arctic? And what about Sam's last day? Did he do or say anything that could possibly provide a clue about what happened later? Was the burnt paper found in his wastebasket an aborted suicide note or something else that might be important?

Are there things that I saw or heard that night that I'm not remembering? And, finally, will the answers to these questions make things better or worse? There's a part of me that wants to shut this down right now and another part of me that can hear Sam saying, "The only thing worse than having fears is not facing them." I vow to dig into my memory bank, leave no stone unturned, and to try to accept whatever I uncover.

FIVE

My gut says that Sam didn't *choose* to end his life. Then again, I'm not a hundred percent positive that I can still trust my inner voice. It's very possible that this feeling in my core is nothing more than my need to protect Sam's character and my memory of who he was and what he stood for. But, for now anyway, I'm listening to my gut, and it's telling me to have faith in my own intuition.

Grabbing my birthday journal off my desk, I sit down on my bed and let "My Journey" begin. Here's whom I'll need to talk to, in no particular order:

Adam and Chase—find out if they heard Sam say or do anything suspicious or unusual in the day or days leading up to his death. Had they ever seen that belt before?

Skip—track him down and find out WTF happened

to him and why he left without saying anything to my parents or, more importantly, *me*. Then ask him if anything unusual happened at school that day. Also ask how upset Sam was about being grounded and missing his party. And see if he knew if anything was going on with Jenny.

Jenny—her number was the last call Sam made from his cell phone, about thirty-five minutes before we found him. What did they talk about? Why had they broken up a month earlier? Was their break-up more serious than Sam made it out to be? Was she possibly pregnant?

Pizza delivery guy—track him down and find out if he saw anyone lurking around our house that night.

??

I look back over the list. *Fuck.* This is going to be extremely painful. Julie's going to be my partner in this investigation, but only in theory. When it comes right down to it, I'm the one who'll need to talk to each of these people, and that's going to totally suck.

I spend the rest of the night catching up on homework and studying for upcoming tests. It's strange, but now that I have some direction in my life—a plan, a purpose, a cause—it's making it way easier to study. I guess I *care* again. Maybe if I work really hard and talk to my teachers about extra credit assignments, I'll be able to get my GPA back up before the semester ends.

On the bus the next morning, I show the list to Julie. "You're not questioning your parents?" she asks.

"No. They weren't with Sam at all his last day until after school when they grounded him and then not again till after the accident, and for most of that time I was in the room with them. Plus, Dad wouldn't be happy that I'm doing this, and Mom, well, she'd be okay with what we're doing if she was her old self. But in her current state, I'm not sure how she'd react, and I can't risk setting her back."

"Got it. So, who do you want to talk to first and what do you want me to do?" she asks.

I look at the list. "I'll talk to Chase the next chance I get," I say. "And Jenny, too, but I hardly ever see her at school, and I don't have her cell. Wish I'd kept Sam's phone records, but I didn't."

"Wait. How did you get Sam's phone records?" Julie says, looking at me sideways.

"After I ditched you, I started really obsessing about everything. I convinced myself that if I could get my hands on all the reports, I'd find something that everyone had missed.

"What were you able to get?"

"The EMT and hospital records, his police file, the autopsy report, and his phone records."

"Did your parents help you?" Julie asks, looking very confused.

"No, I filled out a bunch of forms, forged their names, and waited till they came in the mail."

"Weren't you afraid your parents would see them when they picked up the mail?"

"I'm the only person who bothers getting the mail now."

"I'm very impressed. You're a better sleuth than I'd imagined," Julie says, nodding. "Anyway, Jenny's on my sister's volleyball team. They practice in Baxter Gym and usually end around four on days they don't have games. The schedule is on our kitchen bulletin board, so I can let you know what days this week they'll be practicing."

"Perfect. Why don't you also reach out to John's Pizza and see if you can find out who delivered our pizza and ask them if they saw anything."

"I'm on it. Anything else? What about Skip? Have you talked to him?"

"No, and it makes no sense. He didn't attend Sam's funeral, he hasn't been to our house since Sam's death, and I never see him at school." I take a deep breath and decide to say what's most upsetting. "Do you think he's avoiding me or my family for some reason?"

Julie jerks her head up. "Wait, you don't *know*?" Julie asks, surprised.

"Know what?"

"A few days after Sam died, Skip had some sort of break-down. I heard he was even in a hospital for a while. Now, he's supposedly attending a boarding school somewhere out East. His uncle is headmaster there, wherever *there* is."

My heart starts beating a mile a minute. I don't know if it's because I'm angry or worried—probably some combination of the two. "Holy shit. Why don't I know this?"

"You were in such a deep fog back then, I'm not surprised you didn't hear us all talking about him."

"Wow. All these months I've been calling his cell, but it always goes straight to voicemail. Still, I never imagined that he'd *left* town. I just thought he was trying to avoid me."

"Why would he avoid you?"

To justify Skip's absence, I'd convinced myself that he couldn't face me because he didn't want to risk causing me any more pain. I shrug. "No one wants to be around me," I say, to deflect the focus from Skip. "When I walk down the hall, kids move to the other side. They treat me like I have a horribly toxic and contagious disease. I honestly feel like a leper."

Julie puts her arm around my shoulder. "Bean, I don't think they're trying to be mean. They probably just don't know what to say."

"Whatever. But back to Skip. It still doesn't make sense, that after all this time, he's never once reached out to us. He was so close to our whole family. How could he just ghost us like this?"

Julie's posture stiffens, and I can tell she feels defensive toward Skip. "Is it possible he spoke to your parents, and they forgot to tell you?" she asks hopefully.

"No way. If Skip called, they'd tell me."

Julie looks away, swallows, and looks back at me. "You should probably call his mom, and the sooner the better. Have you noticed they have a For Sale sign in their yard?"

When I get home from school, I go to my room, lock the door, and call Skip's house. My heart is pounding. Mrs. Miller answers on the second ring. They must not have caller ID because she seems shocked when I tell her who I am.

"Well—hello, Bean. What can I do for you?"

"I was hoping to speak to Skip. Does he have a new cell number? I've been trying the number I have, but it always goes straight to voicemail."

There's a long, uncomfortable silence before she finally answers. "He's away, dear. Is there anything *I* can help you with?"

"Away where?" I ask.

"He's attending a boarding school in Connecticut."

"But why?" I blurt. "I never heard him talk about wanting to go to *boarding school*."

"We all thought it best, Bean. He wasn't doing well after Sam passed, and we felt a change of scenery might help him get back on track."

"Is it working?" I ask. I sound sarcastic, but I can't help it—it's how I feel. As if all one had to do to get back on track after losing their best friend was simply to move away.

"It's too soon to know for sure," she says. She sighs. "Listen, Bean, I've got my hands full over here. I don't know if you heard, but Mr. Miller's been transferred to North Carolina, and I've only got a few weeks to get this entire house packed up. If there's nothing else, I should get back to it."

"Does Skip have a new cell number? Because I really need to speak with him."

She lets out another long, drawn-out sigh. "I don't think that's a wise idea. He's not ready."

He's not ready? What about me? What about my family? "Could you at least tell him I called and let him know that whenever he's ready, I'd really love to hear from him?"

"I'll relay your message when I feel it's appropriate to do so," Mrs. Miller says very coldly, as if my only intention is to inflict further pain on Skip.

I wish her luck on their move, but when I hang up, all I really want to do is run over to her house and throttle her. She seemed to have no sympathy for me or my family, and she made Skip sound like some fragile, wounded animal who just needs some separation and a bit of rest. I'd like to know who this wimpy person she's referring to is and what happened to my studly Skip.

That night, Dad picks up Chinese take-out on his way home from work. When I go to ask Mom what she wants on her plate, she says she'll be joining us. I'm not sure if this is 1) some sort of miracle, or 2) she's just trying to prove to me that she's improving, or 3) she's worried I'll break my promise and tell Dad about the pills. In any case, it's nice to have her join us at the table. Nice, but awkward, because dinnertime is when Dad and I discuss what needs to be done around the house and who'll be doing what. With her there, we're both pretty quiet, because we don't want her to know just how much we're both doing to pick up her slack. Instead, we mostly talk about some new electrical component Dad has designed that he'll be presenting to the bigwigs in Chicago the following week. Mom doesn't say much, just a few encouraging words here and there. It didn't look like she'd showered, but her hair is combed and put back in a ponytail, and she appears to be wearing clean sweats, so that's something. Afterwards, she even helps me clean up the dishes and wrap up the leftovers before retreating back to her cave.

After she leaves, I go down to the basement to switch out a load of washing and fold the clothes from the dryer. When I walk back upstairs about a half hour later, Dad and Chase are sitting at the kitchen table. Chase has just returned from hockey practice, and he's eating our leftovers. Dad's sitting next to him. I know I've interrupted something important from the way both of their heads shoot up when I walk in.

"Why don't you put the laundry down and talk with us for a minute," Dad says.

I sit as directed. "What's going on?" I ask, confused.

"I wanted you to know that on Saturday I'm going to be

packing up Sam's things. If there's anything you want of his, please take it before then."

I'm shaking, and I want to scream, but words won't form. Dad and Chase stare at me. They obviously weren't expecting this reaction and, at first, even I don't know why this news is so horribly upsetting. But then I figure it out. This can't happen for two reasons: Removing his things will mean he's never coming back, and though I know how absolutely irrational that sounds, it's the way I feel. And two, there may be clues in their room that we won't ever find if his things are disturbed.

Of course, I can't admit to either of these or they'll send me straight to the loony bin. All I can manage to blurt out is "But why now?"

They look at each other in an *I told you so* sort of way. "It's time, Bean," Dad says flatly.

"But what will you do with his stuff?" I ask.

"I'll box up the important items and store them in the attic, and the rest I'll give to charity."

Important items? As if Dad has a clue what's important. Before I dare say anything I'll regret, I push back my chair and flee. I slam my bedroom door and lean against it with all my weight, feeling like it's me against the world. Tears are streaming down my face, and I honestly feel like I might throw up. A few minutes later there's a knock at my door. "Sis, can I come in?" Chase asks. I wipe my tears with my sleeve and reluctantly open my door.

He walks slowly into my room and then turns around and

shuts the door behind him. "Bean, why are you so upset?" he asks. He's such a loser. He has absolutely no clue about anything.

"Are you trying to erase Sam from our lives? Is that what this is all about?" I ask.

He frowns. "What? Of course not, but it's been over four months. How long do *you* think we should wait?"

"You think that once we get rid of all his possessions, everything will magically return to normal?"

"No, of course not. But it's creepy living in that room with all his stuff everywhere. You never come in, so you don't know what it's like."

"No, *you're* the one that doesn't know what it's like! Why do you think I can't go in there?"

"No clue. Maybe because he's the only one of us you ever gave a shit about."

"That's not true. It's because I was *here*. I saw him. I know how he looked. I know everything that happened in your room, and *you* don't know anything because *you* weren't here. By the time you went in your room, everything had been cleaned up."

"Let me get this straight. You're angry because we were *out* that night?"

"Of course not. I don't care where the fuck you were. I'm just saying there's a reason I don't go in your room."

He nods slowly. "Okay, whatever, but I still don't understand why you don't want us to box up his stuff."

"It's no use. I can't make you understand."

He turns to leave but then suddenly turns back around. "You know, Bean, you're not the only one who lost a brother."

"I never said I was."

"No, but you act like it. Just because I'm able to carry on with my life doesn't mean that I don't miss him and feel just as bad as you do that he isn't with us anymore."

I roll my eyes. "Maybe I've *misunderstood*," I say, totally sarcastically. Because I do believe that I loved Sam on a level Chase couldn't begin to imagine.

"Yeah, Bean, you have. You misunderstand a lot of things. You might have been closer to him than Adam and I were, but that doesn't mean we didn't love him. We had our differences, but we were brothers. We shared a room, but we shared a lot more than that. I really miss him, and I feel his loss deeply. But if it's okay with you, I would like to not be reminded every second I'm in our room about how he died."

No longer able to hold in the fact that I have reservations about the cause of Sam's death, I blurt out, "How *do* you think he died?"

"Is this a trick question?" Chase asks, glaring at me as if I'm a crazy person. "I think we're all pretty clear about that."

"Well, *I'm* not, and I'm going to *prove* that it wasn't a suicide."

Chase raises his eyebrows in disbelief. "I think it was pretty obvious what happened, but I'd love to hear your theory. What do *you* think happened?"

"I don't know. I'm still trying to figure it out. But I know

Sam wouldn't have taken his life," I say, sounding way more confident than I feel. "It wasn't even his belt, right? Had you ever seen that belt?"

"I don't know anything about the belt because, as you pointed out, I wasn't here."

"It was a creepy green camouflage belt. It definitely wasn't his."

He laughs. "All those Nancy Drew books you used to read have done a number on your head."

I feel my face redden. I don't appreciate that he's not taking me seriously. "I don't know why you think this is funny. I just care enough to want to set the record straight."

"I care, too. I guess you don't believe that, but I do. Trust me, I wish his death had been anything but a suicide, but we have to live with the facts, not with what we wish. Do Mom and Dad know you're playing detective? Because I don't think they'd be comfortable with it."

"Please don't tell them. I don't want to cause them any more pain. I just want to see if there's another explanation. If I can't figure it out pretty quickly, I'll give up. Please promise me you won't mention this," I say, suddenly feeling extremely defensive.

"My lips are sealed," he says, gesturing like he's zipping up his mouth.

I breathe a huge sigh of relief. "Thanks. And now that you know what I'm doing, can I please ask you a few questions about his last day?"

"I guess so, but as you just said, I wasn't here, so I doubt I'll be of much help."

"I know, I'm wondering about earlier that day. Did he say anything out of the ordinary or act strangely in any way that you remember?"

"Strange how?" Chase asks, frowning.

"Was he upset about anything?"

"He was very pissed off. I think you know that. He wanted to go to Skip's party. He thought it was stupid that Mom wouldn't let him write his English paper over the weekend, given that he had till Monday to turn it in."

"Anything besides that?"

Chase shrugs. "Seriously, what is the point of all this? Don't you think we're all better off just moving on? No matter how many questions you ask, you're never going to be able to figure out why he did it. If there was another explanation—and trust me, I wish there was—it would have already surfaced."

"Well, I believe you're wrong. I think it's very possible that someone else was involved."

"Really?" he says, raising his eyebrows. "What do you know that I don't know?"

I shrug. "Nothing yet. It's just a feeling I have."

"I guess you gotta do what you gotta do, but I can't help you. I honestly don't know anything more than I've already told you. He seemed perfectly fine before school, and the only thing he seemed upset by that night was having to write that paper."

I nod.

He turns and puts his hand on the door handle, but then swivels his head back around. "So, can we clean out his stuff Saturday, or do you want me to tell Dad that we should wait? If it's really important to you, I'm okay to put it off a while longer."

I guess it isn't really fair of me to prolong this any longer. I can only imagine that being in that room with all of Sam's stuff would be pretty hard. I definitely couldn't do it. "No, it's okay. But before then can I have like an hour in your room by myself while I figure out what I want to keep?"

"Sure. I'll be at my hockey game from nine until at least noon on Saturday, and both Adam and Dad will be with me."

"Adam's coming home this weekend?" I ask, surprised, because he hasn't been home since Christmas break.

"Yeah, he's going to meet us at my game and stay over on Saturday night."

He turns to leave, and suddenly I don't want him to go. "Chase, I'm really sorry if I've been kinda bitchy or whatever. Even though you guys didn't seem all that close, I know that you loved Sam."

He nods. "I did. In fact, I go to his grave every week. Do you ever go?" he asks with a raised eyebrow.

I shake my head. This doesn't seem like the time to explain to Chase that Sam didn't want his body to be in a casket, seven feet underground, or that although I am not sure exactly where his soul is, I am absolutely certain it isn't hanging around that cemetery. "You should go sometime. You'd enjoy seeing the flowers that get delivered every week and reading all the cool stuff kids write to him. It's really pretty amazing."

I suppose I should feel happy to know that Sam touched so many people's lives, but in all honesty, I don't. I guess I don't really want to share him with anyone right now, at least not anyone outside my family. I know how awful this sounds, but it's true.

When I don't reply, Chase says, "I'd be happy to give you a ride out there sometime."

"No, thanks," I say. "I'm not a big fan of cemeteries."

He starts to speak and then stops. He probably wants to say that cemeteries aren't his favorite places either, but he refrains.

Moving closer, I lean into him and let my head drop on his shoulder. "I'm sorry I'm such a brat sometimes. I promise I don't mean to be."

He wraps his arms around me and pulls me in closer. "It's okay. I understand. This is difficult for all of us. Maybe when everything gets cleaned up, you'll come in and hang out with me more. It's just the two of us at home now, and we shouldn't be strangers."

I nod and look up at him. "I will, Chase. I promise." We hug, and then he leaves. It's maybe the first real hug we've ever shared, which is incredibly sad. I walk over and sit on my bed, feeling like a real shit. I think I'm so smart, such a great reader of people, but in reality, I can't even clearly see my own family. I wonder what else I might be refusing to see.

I should get to my homework, but instead I call Julie to tell her about these latest developments.

"I understand why you're upset, but I bet you'll feel better when this is over. Plus, we need to see if there's anything in their room that might help us. Like a clue or something," Julie says.

"You mean a suicide note, don't you?" I say, as this is definitely my worst fear. Finding one would crush me. It would prove I had no clue who Sam was.

"No, of course not. If there was one, the detectives for sure would have found it. People who write suicide notes don't hide them. What would be the point?"

"I hear you, but I still—"

"Put that thought out of your head," she says.

If only I could.

SIX

On the bus to school, Julie says, "After I talked to you last night, I talked to John at John's Pizza. He was nice, but I think that's a dead end. He looked up his records, and a guy named Randy Bravo had the routes in our neighborhood that evening. But he quit that night. Never even came in to pick up his last paycheck. John later mailed it to the address listed on his application, but it came back stamped *Undeliverable: No Such Address*."

"Weird. Who does that?" I ask.

"According to John, lots of his drivers do for one reason or another. Randy delivered the pizzas he had in his car and that was the last John ever heard from him."

"Did he give you his cell number?"

"Yeah, he didn't want to at first, but I weaseled it out of him. I called it, and it went straight to voicemail. The message wasn't in English, but I still left a message. I seriously doubt he'll call back."

"Seems kind of strange that he quit the *same* night?"

Julie shrugs. "Maybe, maybe not."

After school, I go see my algebra teacher, Mr. Gunderson, who's agreed to help me study for an upcoming test. I've been able to catch up pretty quickly in most of my classes, but algebra is a different story. He greets me at the door and tells me to pull a chair up to his desk. When I sit down, I tell him that I'm sorry I've been so checked out and assure him that I'm now focused and completely motivated to learn this stuff. He seems relieved to hear this.

We get to work, and when I finally look up at the classroom clock, I realize we've been at it for over two hours. "I'm really sorry I've taken up so much of your time," I say. "This has been hugely helpful, though. I can take it from here."

He nods. "You're a very smart girl. I had no doubt that if you focused, it would come easily to you."

I try to ignore the *smart girl* bit, because it sounds like he's saying, "For a *girl*, you're pretty smart," but I don't think he is. He's not that kind of guy. I stand up and start stuffing my notes into my backpack.

"Bean, I also wanted to tell you that I'm sorry for your loss, and I completely understand why you've had a tough time this semester. I lost a sister in a similar manner a few years ago. She wasn't nearly as young as Sam, but it was a big shock nonetheless."

I nod, as if I understand what he's talking about. As if I'm in the Siblings of Suicides Club right along with him.

When I get outside, I realize I've missed the late bus. I'd love to walk the mile and a half to my house because I could really use some fresh air, but it's starting to sleet, and it's already getting dark. March twenty-first might mark the first day of spring in other places, but in northern Minnesota it's generally delayed by about a month. Which is a shame because I think longer days and warmer, sunnier weather might help improve my outlook.

I check the hockey schedule and see that Chase has an away game, so, reluctantly, I text Dad. He says he'll be right over. I feel bad bothering him, but I know he'd be mad if he found me walking on the road. While I'm sitting on the curb in the circle in front of our high school waiting, Richie pulls up in his family's '52 green Ford pickup.

"Hey, Bean. You need a lift?" he asks casually, as if we're friends and speak to each other all the time.

I stare at him for like a full minute, feeling horribly awkward. My self-imposed seclusion has made me forget how to be *me*. I've known who he was forever—but from a distance. Knowing that he might like me changes everything. Plus, he is so *hot*. How could he possibly be interested in me? To be honest, I'm pretty cute, but I'm a freshman, and he's a junior—a very popular junior. Finally, after what feels like the longest, most uncomfortable silence of my life, I manage to say, "Thanks, but my dad's on his way."

"Okay. Would you like some company while you wait? I could park and hang out with you."

I shrug. "Um, sure. I guess." I'm totally humiliated. I sound like a bumbling idiot. But maybe he doesn't notice, because he parks across from me in the parking lot, and then walks back over and sits next to me on the curb.

"I don't want to make this weird or anything, but I want to say I'm really sorry about Sam. I wanted to say something to you at the funeral—"

"You were there?" I actually have little memory of Sam's funeral, except I definitely know Skip *wasn't* there.

He nods. "Every hockey player at the school went, but I would have gone even if I wasn't with my team. It was hard for me, so I can't imagine what it must have been like for you and your family. I saw you, and I felt I should say something, but I didn't know what the right thing to say was."

"That's okay," I say, and I mean it. Even though I feel incredibly nervous and awkward around him, I'm relieved that he mentioned Sam's name. No one else does, so his name hangs silently and uncomfortably in the air. "It was a weird day," I say. "Not at all what Sam would have wanted." Richie gives me a strange look, and I realize how deranged I sound. "I just mean that he was into Inuit stuff, and they do things more naturally. He wouldn't have wanted that whole scene at the funeral home and especially not the casket," I say.

Dad's car pulls in, which is a bummer. I'd like to get to

know Richie better so I could stop feeling so awkward around him. He was sweet to hang out with me. But I'm also relieved, as I feel incredibly self-conscious, and I'm sure I'll say something even more stupid than I already have if I don't get out of here quick. Guess I'm out of practice talking to anyone of the opposite sex. "This is my dad, so I better go." I stand up, and Richie does too.

"I'm glad we finally talked," he says.

"Yeah, thanks for hanging out with me."

"Sure. See you around," he says. Before he walks away, he gives me an adorable smile, which totally melts me.

"Was that Matt Branson's son you were speaking to?" Dad asks when I slide into the car.

"Yeah, his name's Richie. He's a JV hockey player."

Dad nods and tries to act cool, like seeing me with a boy is totally normal. "Right, I heard he's quite good."

"That's what people say, but I wouldn't know. I've never seen him play." Dad's listening to his favorite news and weather station, and we both listen to the weatherman say, "It's sleeting now, but by midnight a warm front will be passing through, and by commute time tomorrow the sun will be shining and temperatures will finally reach into the low forties. Let's all pray that spring is just around the corner, because we've sure had ourselves a doozy of a winter."

"Amen," Dad says. "Hopefully, the lake won't be frozen much longer. I've noticed it's thinning along the shore."

I feel a wave of panic. The predicted ice melt date is big news in northern Minnesota, where our lives revolve almost entirely around water. In the warm months we swim, boat, and fish, and when the lakes freeze over, we skate, ice fish, and play hockey. Usually I'm psyched for the ice melt, as our winters are long and brutal. But not this year, because when the ice melts, the doe will sink into the lake's deep abyss, and I'll lose forever the one thing that somehow feels connected with Sam. Suddenly, it feels like a race against time to figure out how Sam died.

"Is something wrong?" Dad says, startling me.

"No."

"You sure?"

"Yes." But after a few minutes I can't hold it in any longer. "Okay, so there's a doe frozen into the lake beside our dock, and I guess I don't want her to fall into the water when the ice melts. Which I know sounds crazy, but that's how I feel."

"This is that doe you put all those rocks and boards around?" he asks.

I nod, somewhat shocked that he knows this fact, as I haven't seen him go out to our backyard all winter. "How did you know about that?"

"I saw it a while back when I was shoveling snow off the roof. Chase said he thought you'd put them there. What made you do that, Bean?"

I take a deep breath. I don't really want to tell him why I believe the doe is important, because I suspect he already thinks

I'm a bit crazy, but the weight of all the secrets I've been keeping has become too heavy for me to handle. "I know this will sound strange, but that doe appeared on the ice the night we had our accident, and I think she might be the same deer we hit."

Dad looks at me. "I've been meaning to apologize to you."

"For what?" I ask.

"The mechanic who repaired my Mustang told me he found deer hair embedded in the front grille. I'm sorry I didn't believe you. Guess I was pretty wound up about my car, and then when I couldn't find the deer that night, well, I just figured you were lying to protect Sam. Can you accept my apology?"

I nod.

"I should have said something earlier, but you know me, I don't like to be wrong."

"It's okay, Dad."

"Well, thanks. Now, tell me how you suppose this dead deer got all the way from the street to the lake."

"Maybe it wasn't dead—just stunned or something. And then it recovered enough to get up, but then it only made it as far as the lake."

Dad pulls into the driveway and abruptly stops the car. "That sounds pretty preposterous, even for you, but let's say you're right. Why build a barrier around it?"

"Remember I told you that after our accident, Sam, because of his Inuit beliefs, mixed his blood with hers to appease its soul?"

"Yes."

"Well, if this is the same deer, then she's sacred. It's like she and Sam are somehow connected and always will be."

Dad doesn't say a thing. He just stares straight ahead.

"You think I'm crazy, don't you?" I ask.

He finally turns to face me. "It's not important whether or not *I* believe you. What's important is what *you* believe. You know I've had a lot of time to think about all this—about Sam and his Inuit beliefs and his certainty that everything had a deeper meaning. What I've come to understand is that you and Sam, and your mother, see things much differently than I do. I always thought my way was right, and you were all a bit off, but I suppose I was being arrogant and, well, maybe even a bit igno-rant. The truth is that we each view the world through our own unique lenses. I have a hard time seeing out of your lenses, and you probably have an equally difficult time seeing out of mine, but we can choose to accept our differences." He unfastens his seatbelt. "The hard part is that I can't help but wonder if Sam would still be with us if I'd come to this understanding sooner. That thought haunts me."

I'm staring at Dad in total disbelief. His words don't sound anything like him, yet they're coming out of his mouth. "No, Dad. Please don't think that."

"I can't help it. You'd all been in an obviously traumatic acci-dent, Sam was a soaking-wet, bloody mess, and he looked like he was in shock or God knows what, and what did I do? I didn't listen to how the accident happened or why Sam was so messed up. I was just feeling angry and embarrassed. I was more concerned with the way it all must have looked to our friends than with my own children's well-being. Instead of providing comfort and love, I screamed, ranted, and accused you all of lying. What the hell was I thinking?"

I swallow hard. My dad sounds like he's evolved into a different person. I don't recognize his voice or his contrition. But in any case, I love what I'm hearing. I pat him on the back and smile. "It doesn't matter anymore, Dad. It's in the past, and we all have to try to grow from the experience and move forward."

"I'd love to move forward, but it's hard when I feel that I might be responsible for my son's death. Maybe I upset him so much that he lost it."

His eyes begin filling with tears. I've never seen him cry before. Not even at Sam's funeral. He's always been the strong one who doesn't show much emotion, and I'm finding it hard to see him so vulnerable. I lean over the console farther and wrap my arms around him. Then I release him and look him in the eye. "Sam wasn't that fragile. You were kind of a jerk that night, but you definitely didn't cause his death. So, please put that thought out of your mind."

"But—"

"No, seriously, it's not your fault. I promise." I'm lying, and he knows it. That's one of the hardest parts of Sam's leaving. Because no one understands why it happened or, in my case, who's responsible, each of us is shouldering our own guilt. The *what-ifs* just keep piling up, each of us believing that if we'd acted in a certain way or done something differently, Sam would still be with us. I don't think Dad's words played a part in Sam's death, but I can't be a hundred percent certain that they didn't, and he knows that.

He smiles a fake smile, and we go back to our guilt-ridden lives.

After class on Thursday, I head over to Baxter Gym to wait for volleyball practice to end. After spotting Jenny through the small gym windows, I drop my coat on the floor near the wall between the gym and the locker room and sit down on top of it to wait for her. I figure I'll spend the next hour finishing my homework, but when I open my American History textbook, I find it impossible to concentrate. I can't imagine how I'm going to ask a girl I barely know about her relationship with my dead brother. I know he was really smitten with her in a way he hadn't been with other girlfriends, most of whom came and went so quickly I never bothered to learn their names. But Jenny was different. She came to our house fairly often and even had dinner with us a handful of times, though not once did I have a one-on-one conversation with her. As far as I could tell, they seemed like a good match. She enjoyed hiking and fishing, which the others had absolutely no interest in. When she stopped coming around, I wanted to ask Sam what had happened, but I didn't think it was any of my business. And now, here I am waiting to confront Jenny about it, which feels beyond wrong.

At ten after four, the doors open, and the team walks en masse toward the locker room. Jenny's in the middle of the pack, talking to someone I don't recognize. I hate to interrupt her, but if I don't, I'll miss my opportunity.

I call her name, and she stops talking and looks in my direction and then moves out of the pack with her friend. She looks nervous, tentative. "Bean, hi," she says.

"Hi. Could I please talk to you for a few minutes?" I ask.

She turns back to her friend and says something I can't hear, then her friend leaves, and soon we are the only two left in the hallway. "How are you? And how's your family? I should've called after the funeral. And now, so much time has passed."

I smile. "It's okay. It's been really difficult, but I guess we're doing pretty good, or as well as can be expected."

"Good. I'm relieved to hear that."

I look down at the floor and start shifting my weight from one foot to the other, trying to decide how to begin.

Finally, she says, "Did you want to talk to me about something?"

"Yes. Sorry, I know this is weird but I'm just trying to figure out if there's anything that was missed," I blurt out.

"Do you mean missed by the detective? Because I told him everything I know."

I'm shocked. "You talked to the detective?" The records in Sam's police file did not have any information about them contacting Jenny. I imagine they got her name and number from Sam's phone records, but I'm startled to hear that they not only reviewed these records, but they actually spent time tracking her down.

She hesitated and noticeably lowered her voice. "Yeah, they came to my house like the next day, or no, it was actually that Monday. They were waiting at my house when I came off the bus. I guess I was the last person Sam talked to that night, at least by phone."

I could tell that whatever they'd talked about had bothered her or maybe was *still* bothering her. I felt weird asking about it, but I had to know. "If you don't mind my asking, why did Sam call you?"

"He wanted to know if I'd read *The Things They Carried*, which I hadn't. He told me he had to write a paper, and if he couldn't get it done, then he couldn't go to Skip's party."

"What did you say?"

"I hadn't read it, but I promised to ask some friends and get back to him."

"And did you?"

Her eyes well up and her shoulders sag. "No," she says, looking at the ground. "I got caught up in some stupid friend drama and completely forgot about it. It wasn't until I got to Skip's and didn't see him that I remembered that I'd totally left him hanging." Her head snaps up, and she quickly covers her mouth with both hands. "Oh, God! I'm sorry. I didn't mean—"

It's actually quite shocking how often this happens. Stupid little idioms, spoken with absolutely no malice, now have a sinister undertone. Phrases like "Hang in there," or "He was at the end of his rope," or "That was really below the belt" have the effect of a stab to the heart. I take a deep breath. "It's okay, really. I know you didn't. Was there anything else you told the detective?"

"Yeah, they asked what my relationship with Sam was, and I told him that we'd dated for a couple of months starting in the fall, but that we'd recently broken up."

"Did they ask why you broke up?"

"I didn't really go into it, but I explained that it was no big deal, and that we'd remained good friends."

I decide to go to the thing I most want to know. "Was that true that it was no big deal, or was there more to it? I mean, why did you guys end it? Did something happen?" Jenny looks taken aback so I quickly add, "I'm sorry. I swear I don't think your breakup had anything to do with his death. I'm just curious, I guess. It's totally cool if you don't want to tell me. It's really none of my business."

"It's okay," she says. "It was nothing dramatic. We realized that we were two very different people. I wanted to be more like him, a free spirit, willing to try anything, but then one night my parents caught me trying to sneak out to meet him, and I guess it made me realize that I wasn't quite up for the adventure of dating Sam, if you know what I mean."

"No, not really. Was he trying to get you to do something bad, like drugs?"

"Oh, no, nothing like that. As far as I know, no one in our

group has done much besides pot and drinking." She pauses, and I see her struggling. "What I was really referring to was sex," she says.

I feel so uncomfortable I want to die. This is way too personal, but I asked for it. And a big part of me wants to know.

Thankfully, Jenny ends the uncomfortable silence. "I wasn't ready, and he was. But it was all cool. We talked about it, and we mutually decided to end our relationship. It was no big deal. We both realized, independently, that we were just meant to be friends."

So, the good news is that Sam's death had nothing to do with Jenny being pregnant, which is one of the million things I've considered. But I'm still not clear if she means that they were both virgins or if only she was. It probably sounds absurd, but for some reason, I don't want Sam to have died without having had sex. That just sounds wrong—for anyone. Not that I know what I'm talking about. But Sam did talk about how he thought people were really messed up about sex. I remember him saying that it was such a natural, beautiful act, but our society had twisted it around and somehow made it seem nasty and dirty. "Was Sam a virgin?" I ask.

She laughs. "I'm not sure I should be telling you this, but I guess it can't do any harm at this point. No, Sam was not a virgin. He'd gone all the way with at least two girls that I know of, and there could be more. As you probably know, a lot of girls were into him."

I feel a flush of embarrassment and then a wave of insecurity. Here was a thing I didn't know about Sam, a whole part of his life that was kept secret from me. If he could keep something this big from me, then what else didn't I know about him? But I can't think about that right now. I'm just happy he didn't die a virgin, that he got to experience what he told me was one of life's greatest joys. "Is there anything else you told the detective?" I ask.

"I told them about the book report and that Sam was mad that he might not be able to attend Skip's party, but surely not *suicidal* mad, which is what they seemed to be insinuating."

"You said that?"

She nods.

"You don't think he killed himself?" I ask.

She shrugs. "I don't know, Bean," she says. "I sure didn't see it coming. Makes absolutely no sense."

"Do you have any theories?"

"I wish I did. I can't believe he would take his own life, but I also can't imagine who would want to harm him."

"Do you know anyone who had a green camouflage belt?"

Jenny frowns. "No, why?"

"That's what was around his neck. It wasn't his. I know it wasn't. Part of me thinks that if I can find out whose belt it is, we'll have the killer."

"Definitely not his style, but a lot of guys wear full camouflage gear during deer season so they can go hunting directly after school. And it was deer season then, so that type of belt hardly narrows things down."

"I guess you're right. One last question. Do you know if the detective talked to anyone besides you?"

Jenny nods. "He asked me if I knew how they could reach Skip. I guess his number and my number were the only calls Sam made that night. They said they'd tried to reach him, but he hadn't returned their calls. I explained that I'd heard Skip had had a breakdown and was in a hospital. I told them I thought it best that they not speak to him given the situation, and I also told them that we were all with Skip at his party that entire night, so it was unlikely he'd be able to provide any helpful information."

I nod, but I wonder if this is true. Sam told me that they'd invited nearly everyone in their class, so there were probably at least seventy or eighty kids crowded into a two-car garage. I think it's entirely possible that Skip could have left, for a short period of time anyway, without anyone missing him. I don't want to believe that he could have anything to do with Sam's death, but there's something about him being MIA that isn't sitting well with me. If I could talk to him, I'd feel a whole lot better. But who knows when, or if, that will ever happen. "Okay, well, thanks for talking to me."

"You're welcome, Bean. Only wish I could have been more helpful."

When she walks away, I put on my coat, toss my books into my backpack, and head toward the late buses. Once I'm inside, I rest my arms across the back of the seat in front of me and lower my head onto my arms. I feel kind of sick. Jenny was yet another dead end. I'm ticking people off my list, but I'm getting absolutely nowhere. I can't help but wonder if this isn't a big waste of time. I'm afraid to admit this because being on this journey has allowed me to shed the heavy weight of gloom I'd been living under. It's given me purpose and hope. But that hope is dwindling by the day. And without hope, what do I really have?

As soon as my head hits the pillow that night, thoughts begin to pile up, causing my head to spin out of control. For one thing, I'm dreading going into the boys' room. I don't know if I'm ready to see that hideous chin-up bar, Sam's possessions, his empty bed, and anything else incriminating that might be lurking there. I feel such pressure because I don't know what to look for or what I should take, and I'll only have one shot at it. If I miss something, there's a good chance it will be gone forever. Then I start thinking about the doe. Why is she so important to me? I guess because I feel so strongly that she's the same deer we hit, and if it turns out I'm wrong about that, then I'm probably wrong about a lot of things. Though I really have no way to prove this.

And Mom, is she really improving or is it all just an act? I thought it was a good sign that when I went downstairs today after school to do the laundry, it had already been done. But later, when we asked her to join us for dinner, she made some lame excuse, so who knows if she's really on the mend or faking it. There are now only eleven days left before Mom has to come clean to Dad about the pills. How will he react when he finds out? I've also started to really worry about them as a couple. I know the divorce rate skyrockets when a couple loses a child. Can their marriage survive this, especially given that Mom seems to have completely shut him, and everyone else, out of her life?

I feel like I'm standing on very shaky ground. I don't know what's up and what's down. I thought I knew Chase pretty well, but obviously I don't, because never in a million years would I have guessed that he regularly visits Sam's grave or that he regrets that the two of them weren't closer. And Dad? Why hadn't I ever considered how bad he feels about the way he treated Sam or the fact that he expressed more concern for his car than for Sam's well-being that night?

And if I was so wrong about Chase and Dad, could I also be wrong about Sam? Was there something going on his life that he couldn't face? It's hard to imagine, but if I'm being totally honest with myself, the facts are pretty damning. There was no evidence that would indicate that he'd been in a struggle or that anyone, besides family, had been in their room that night. He was six feet and weighed about a hundred and seventy-five pounds, and the only bruises on his body were around his neck and on his chest where he'd cut himself. Plus, if I really believed someone had come into our house and strangled him, shouldn't I be scared to death that his killer is still on the loose? I definitely should be, but I'm not. Even given all the evidence, my gut still tells me there's another explanation, that there's something we're all missing. Or, maybe, this feeling in my gut is nothing more than my desperate wish for there to be another explanation, because I think that's the only thing that would allow us to fully wipe out our collective guilt and allow us to completely heal.

I try and redirect my thoughts to Sam and some of our shared moments and adventures together, because in the end, that's all I have left of him. Instead, all I can conjure up are the times when he asked me to go exploring or fishing or whatever and I turned him down. I didn't know our time together would be cut short, that our future wasn't a sure thing, so there were a lot of times when I *rejected* him. The thought of getting out of my cozy, warm bed at dawn and hopping into a frigid metal boat to fish and listen to more Inuit stories didn't always sound so appealing. But now? I'd give absolutely anything to spend just five more minutes with him, and when he told me Inuit stories, I'd *really* listen. Maybe if I'd listened more intently, I'd have more clarity about Sam's leaving. Maybe somewhere mixed into those stories there were answers that would help me understand his death on a more spiritual level.

Sam, please, if you're listening from wherever you are, can you give me some sign that lets me know I'm doing the right thing in trying to find out what happened to you? Just some assurance that I'm on the right track?

SEVEN

While waiting for the afterschool buses Friday, Julie and a few other friends discuss meeting up at the varsity basketball game later that evening, but I decline, even though Richie told me he'd be there. I'm too wound up about going into the boys' room tomorrow to be social.

I arrive home, toss my backpack in the mudroom, and walk into the kitchen, where I find Mom preparing her famous hot artichoke dip.

"Who are you making the dip for?" I ask, as it's the dish she's famous for bringing to parties.

"Letty's having us over for dinner."

"You're actually going out?"

She nods. "Yes. It will just be the four of us. Very low key. I believe I can handle that. At least I want to try, for your father's sake."

"That's great, Mom." Hearing that she's acknowledging Dad's feelings is a huge relief. I pray it isn't too little, too late.

She rubs my back. "And what're your plans?" she asks.

"I'm going to chill. It's been a long week." I'm not sure she knows we'll be cleaning out Sam's stuff this weekend. If not, I don't want to be the one to tell her.

After my parents leave, I make myself a veggie stir-fry, clean my room, and then head downstairs to deal with the laundry. To my astonishment, I find the basement totally devoid of dirty clothes. There's nothing in the washer or the dryer and even the laundry baskets are empty. Assuming none of Mom's friends had a hand in this, it has to be a sign that she's improving. I don't want to get ahead of myself, but I'm pretty psyched that she's left the house and done laundry all in the same day.

Loser that I am, I get into bed around 9:30, after grabbing *Stuart Little* from the den bookshelf. I need to be reminded about the importance of being fearless, and who better to remind me than Stuart? Sadly, the book doesn't do the trick. I feel scared and also a bit sick to my stomach. I'm not sure if it's nerves or maybe my tummy rumblings are the beginning stages of a stomach flu. I decide to try another book, so I get out of bed and go to the den. I close my eyes and move my hand gently along the spines, hoping something will *feel* right to me, and one finally does. It's called *Mutant Message Down Under*. Strange title, and I've never seen it before or heard anything about it, which is rare as I'm very familiar with the books in our den library. I pull it from the shelf and return to my room. I get back in bed, arrange the pillows in back of me, and open to the first page. A letter addressed to Sam flutters out and lands face-up on my comforter.

December 2019
Dear Sam,

I feel sure that buried deep within you is a love for the written word (beyond those Inuit books of yours!). In fact, I believe reading might not only help keep you out of trouble, but it may help unlock some of your deeper passions. You should explore books by authors like Rachel Carson, Aldo Leopold, and Paul Hawken. This book you're holding is one of my very favorites. It's centered around another native culture, the Australian Aborigines. Some bookstores have it in fiction and others in nonfiction, which is interesting in and of itself. I hope it speaks to you the way it did to me. But if not, I hope you'll keep trying others, and I'm always around to offer more suggestions. Your mind is much too fertile and imaginative to waste. I leave you with this poem by E. A. Robinson, and warm wishes for a very happy holiday season.

Credo

I cannot find my way: there's no star
In all the shrouded heavens anywhere;
And there is not a whisper in the air
Of any living voice but one so far
That I can hear it only as a bar
Of lost, imperial music, played when fair
And angel fingers wove, and unaware,
Dead leaves to garlands where no roses are.

No, there's not a glimmer, nor a call,
For one that welcomes, welcomes when he fears,
The black and awful chaos of the night;
For through it all—above, beyond it all—
I know the far-sent message of the years,
I feel the coming glory of the Light.

Sincerely,
Mrs. Scamehorn, ninth-grade English

I read the poem and the letter at least four times. It must
mean something that of all the books in our library, I chose this
one. Plus, I've never heard of an English teacher by that name.
She must have been gone by the time I got to high school. It
also seems strange that Sam never even mentioned her to me.

WINTER OF THE WOLF

She sounds very cool, and she really stuck her neck out for him, because I know for a fact that school rules prohibit teachers from giving students gifts. What could all this mean? I text Julie to see if she's awake, and she immediately calls.

"What's up? Thought you'd be asleep by now," she says.

"I'm trying, but I guess I'm pretty wound up about tomorrow. Anyway, I wanted to run something by you." I tell her about asking Sam for a sign and then finding the book and the letter and poem from a mysterious teacher.

"Take a pic and send it to me," Julie says. "I want to see it."

I send it to her, and after a few minutes, she says, "Wow!"

"Wow what?" I ask.

"Bean, for a brainiac, you can be a real knucklehead sometimes. It's right there in black and white. 'The black and awful chaos of the night,' meaning your nightmares and misgivings about all this. 'For through it all—above, beyond it all—I know the far-sent message of the years, I feel the coming glory of the Light.' Could it be any clearer? It's basically saying it's the darkest before the dawn. Sam has come through loud and clear. You're not listening!"

"You sure?"

"Yes. Now get to bed. You should sleep really well tonight. You asked, and you received."

"That would sure be nice. Okay, see you tomorrow."

"Night."

I read the book for an hour or so. It's so good, I don't want to put it down. Around midnight, I finally turn off my light and

135

force myself to get to sleep. But it's not happening. The bedsheets tangle around my body as I toss and turn from side to side. I feel like I'm awake more than I'm asleep. Around 3 a.m., I turn on my bedside light and read for an hour or so before falling back to sleep. When I finally wake up, the room is bright. Groggily, I lean over and glance at my bedside clock and see that it's 10:58 a.m. *Shit!* The boys will be back in an hour. I've got to haul my ass out of bed now! I consider skipping the shower, but I need to clear my head. In the hall, I notice that my parents' door is open, and I start to worry that Mom will hear me and need breakfast or something, which I have no time for. But when I glance in their room, not only is she not there, but their bed is made. Could she have gone to Chase's game? That seems impossible.

While standing under the showerhead, trying to collect my thoughts, bits of my last dream come floating back to me. I'm alone in the boys' room, and it feels sort of surreal and cloudy, like the room is full of fog. I'm chilled and shivering. I look around their room and see that the window closest to Sam's bed is wide open; the venetian blinds are cockeyed and the curtains are being blown backwards into the room. I walk over to shut the window, but it won't budge. As these dream images come back to me, I realize that I've had this exact dream before, which must mean something. But what exactly?

Stepping out of the shower, I quickly throw on some jeans and a sweatshirt, brush my teeth and hair, and walk down the hall to the boys' room. "It's now or never," I say. Pushing their door farther open, I'm stunned by the scene before me. Dirty clothes are lying everywhere, papers are scattered over Adam's and Chase's desks, dirty plates and glasses litter nearly every surface, and from the looks of it, their sheets haven't been washed in months. Plus, it smells *bad*—some horrid mixture of rotting food, spoiled milk, stinky socks, and mildewed towels. The entire room is a disaster zone—except for Sam's desk and his perfectly made bed, at the foot of which Dawg is curled up, lightly snoring. It reminds me of those pictures you see on the news of post-tornado trailer parks where there's always one trailer that wasn't touched, and you don't know if you should be happy for the owners or if you should pity them. I drew the line at going into their room to clean, but I would never have imagined they could live in this level of filth and chaos.

I don't want to see it, but my eyes are drawn to the chin-up bar. I'm horrified to see that it's still there. But I suppose it's possible that the boys don't even know that's where we found Sam hanging. And then I notice the window, the same one from my dream. Its blinds are drawn shut, but they're mangled and falling halfway off, and the curtains are badly water stained. It's exactly how it looked in my dream, minus the blowing wind. But what does it mean?

As I walk farther into the room, Dawg lifts her head and wags her tail very slightly. She's a far cry from the vibrant pooch she was a few months back. I sit down beside her, and she rolls over to expose her tummy, her favorite place to be petted. I'm happy to oblige her simple request. Poor girl, I actually feel sorrier for her than I do for myself. After a few minutes, I move up toward the head of the bed, lie down, and roll over so I can bury my face deep into Sam's pillow one last time. Picking up a corner of his plaid Woolrich blanket, I begin to breathe in and out, slowly and deeply. Sam's scent lingers in the fibers, a woodsy combination of cedar and pine from the incense he regularly burned on his nightstand. This is the closest I've felt to him since he left, and it feels heavenly and also unbearably sad. I want to stay here and absorb him longer, but time is ticking by. I stand, straighten the bedding, give Dawg a final pat on the head, and begin looking around the room.

I sit at his desk, take a deep breath, and pray I won't find a suicide note or anything else that might point in that direction. Then I dig in. The top drawer has nothing personal in it, just pens, pencils, rubber bands, some Post-its, and a stapler. The middle drawer contains printer paper and ink cartridges. The bottom drawer is a hodge-podge of mostly weird stuff he's collected over the years, such as tortoise shells, rocks, and old glass bottles. There are also half a dozen packages of condoms. Beneath all this are a bunch of old notebooks. I take them out and flip through them. Thankfully, they appear to contain nothing but class notes. From the looks of it, he started off each class dutifully taking notes and then quickly petered out. I breathe a huge sigh of relief before returning them and shutting the drawer.

I slowly survey the room, wondering what to take. Suddenly, I remember his collection of feathers. That's what I want. He loved birds, and he somehow managed to find the most amazing feathers wherever he went. He had them arranged in a mason jar on his desk, but I don't see it or the feathers anywhere. Weird. I walk over to the closet to see if by chance it's in there, but no luck. The closet does, however, smell like him, so I rummage around and grab his favorite red-and-black plaid flannel work shirt, his old faded and well-worn jean jacket, and his black terrycloth robe. Walking back to his dresser, I locate three of his favorite T-shirts before going back to his bed to grab his pillow and the incense. The clock now says 11:48. I survey the room one last time.

My gut's telling me I'm missing something, but I can't figure out what. I decide to try to channel Sam. I sit back down on his bed and close my eyes. *Sam, if you're here, I could really use your help. Is there something important in here that you want me to have?* I meditate on this thought for a few minutes, but nothing pops into my head. I make my way to the door with everything I've gathered tucked under my arms. On the way out, I accidently bump into the bookshelf, just to the right of their door, and down topple three of Sam's Inuit books. I pick them up off the floor and then find five others on the shelf. *Thank you, Sam!* These books, all rare and mostly out of print, took Sam a long time to collect, and I feel certain Dad would have tossed them out if I hadn't rescued them. I also feel pretty certain that they didn't fall randomly.

I look back at Dawg. What will she do when Sam's bed is removed? "Hey, Dawg, want to go for a walk?" I say enthusiastically.

She lifts her head and wags her tail a few times, then puts her head back down. I guess she wants to soak up every last molecule of Sam while she still can, and who can blame her? When Dad removes this bed, I'll try to get her to sleep in my room. She weighs close to seventy pounds, often smells like wet dog, and was very partial to Sam, but I know he would have wanted me to try harder to gain her affection.

I return to my room and toss everything onto the bed. My stomach feels totally fine now. I guess it wasn't the flu, just my nerves. I call Julie. "It's done. I didn't find anything bad, but I'm not sure I found anything helpful either, except maybe his Inuit books."

She sighs. "That's great. I've been so nervous for you. Do you want me to come over? We could start reading through the books. Or you could bring them here. No one's home."

"They'll all be back from Chase's hockey game soon so I'm going to stick around and try to talk to Adam. This is probably the last time he'll be home before the semester ends."

"Okay. I'll be here if you need anything, and good luck with Adam."

A few minutes later I hear them all walk in the door. I haven't seen Adam in months, yet we barely acknowledge each other. This isn't unusual, but it stings more than usual.

"You missed a great game, Bean. Your brother, here," Dad says, patting Chase's shoulder, "scored the winning goal with five seconds to spare. It was absolutely stunning."

I look over at Chase. "That's awesome. Wish I'd seen it," I say, feeling inexplicably guilty about not attending his game, even though I haven't attended more than a handful since he started playing way back in elementary school.

"Did you take what you wanted of Sam's? Can we start tackling his room now? Thought we'd get on it while we've got Adam to help us," Dad says. Mom, standing beside him, hears this but she doesn't seem anxious or upset. I presume she was already forewarned.

I nod. "The only thing I couldn't find were his feathers. They were in a jar on his desk. Have either of you seen them?" I ask, directing my question to Chase and Adam.

Adam moves around Dad and steps in front of me. "I have them," he says.

"Oh," I say, taken aback. "Why do *you* have them?"

"Because they were important to Sam. Is that a good enough reason?" Adam asks, sounding defensive.

Once again, I've proven how insensitive I am. "Yeah, sure. I'm just surprised, that's all."

Adam abruptly turns and walks away. I retreat to my bedroom and shut my door, feeling out of sorts. Those feathers were one of Sam's prized possessions, so shouldn't I have them and not Adam? That's probably not fair, but I can't help feeling that I should get first dibs.

A few minutes later there's a knock at my door. I open it, and Adam's standing there holding out his cupped hands, in which the feathers are carefully arrayed on top of one of Sam's signature blue bandanas. He lifts his hands up, as if he's presenting them to me.

"You don't want them?" I ask.

"I do want them, but if they're really important to you, I guess I'll find something else."

Now, I officially feel like a total schmuck. A part of me wants to punish my brothers for not being nicer to Sam, but the fact that Adam knew that Sam's feathers were important to him makes me realize that they were closer than I like to admit. "No, you should keep them. It's fine. I just wondered what happened to them."

"You're sure?"

"Yes."

"Do you know why Sam collected feathers?" Adam asks.

"He was really into birds. He thought they were messengers or something like that. It goes back to the Inuit, like pretty much everything did for him."

"And he found all of these around here?" Adam asks, looking down at the huge array of different-colored feathers he's holding. "It's hard to believe we have this many species of birds in Minnesota. All I seem to see are blackbirds and Canada geese."

I laugh. "I know. It was like feathers were always magically falling directly out of the sky and into his hands. I'd watch it happen, but I could rarely find the bird they came from."

Adam smiles. "So, how're you holding up?" he asks. "Chase said you weren't too thrilled about us packing up Sam's stuff."

"At first I wasn't. But I get that that wasn't fair of me. Guess I hadn't considered how weird it's been for you guys to be surrounded with all his things. But I'm onboard with it now. Overall, I think I'm doing at least a little better than I was."

"Good to hear. Chase also said you believe that Sam was murdered. Is that true?"

I swallow hard. I don't want to be having this conversation. At least not with Adam. And I feel betrayed that Chase shared this with him, even though I didn't expressly ask him not to. "I have a very hard time believing that he took his own life. I don't think he was capable of that, nor can I imagine what could have been going on with him that would make him consider doing such a thing. Because if he did it, then I obviously didn't really know him, and that's pretty hard to accept."

"Guess we all feel that way. It sucks that we'll never know."

"I haven't given up yet. I still think it's possible that there's another explanation. Which is why I'm asking a few people some questions. If you don't mind, could I ask you about Sam's last day?"

He looks at me and cocks his head. "What exactly do you want to know?"

"Did anything about that day stick out to you as being different?"

"He and Mom had that blow-up about the assignment he didn't turn in, but besides that, I can't really think of anything."

"How did that all go down with Mom? You guys were in the room when she confronted him, right?"

He nods. "But Bean, come on—I don't really see the relevance."

"Please just tell me what you remember."

He takes a deep breath. "Mom came into our room and asked Sam about a book report. Sam claimed he'd already turned it in, but when Mom said she'd just gotten off the phone with his teacher, he backpedaled and said it was almost complete, and he promised he'd hand it in to his teacher first thing Monday morning. Mom asked to see it, and he gave her some bullshit excuse, explaining that he had it all worked out in his head but hadn't yet written anything. Mom had obviously read the book, and she started asking him specific questions about it, and it was clear, even to me, that Sam hadn't read a word of it. He promised that he'd wake up early and get on it, but Mom said no, he had to start it immediately. Sam explained that he couldn't because he had to get to Skip's to help him set up for the party. That's when she totally lost it and told him he was grounded till it was complete. She said she'd had it with his lies."

"Then what happened?"

"It got pretty ugly. He said something about never forgiving her if he couldn't go to Skip's."

"Shit, really?"

Adam nods.

"Poor Mom. Then what happened?"

"She shut our door, and he hurled a book at it and started calling her names I'd rather not repeat."

I suddenly feel horrified for Mom. I pray that she didn't hear his insults. "Do you think she was being unfair?"

"Hell no. I was proud of her for finally sticking it to him. Let's face it, he was her favorite, and he got away with shit all the time that none of us would have. But I'm sure she feels awful about it. Not exactly how you want to remember your last conversation with your beloved son."

"Thankfully, those weren't their last words. They spoke after our car accident. Or I guess I should say, Mom spoke. Sam didn't say much. But she took care of him, cleaned up his wounds and stuff, and she was very loving and nurturing."

"Oh, good. Makes me feel better for Mom."

"Is there anything else you can remember about that day or night?"

Adam frowns. "Seriously, Bean? Do you honestly think that Chase and I haven't gone over every minute of every day leading up to his death to try and figure out what we might have missed? We shared a room. Maybe we weren't super close, but we still thought we knew him pretty well, or at least knew what we thought he was and wasn't capable of. If we had any idea that he was feeling so low, we would have helped him."

"What do you mean? How?"

"Both Chase and I had written papers on that book. If we'd

given a crap, we could have given them to him. If we had, he could have had the paper finished in an hour or so and been able to go to Skip's. But we didn't. We left him there, mad as hell, and went off to eat pizza and watch some idiotic sci-fi movie. The worst part is that we actually laughed about it. How do you think that makes us feel?"

I drop my head. "Pretty bad, I imagine," I say, understanding for the first time the depth of my brothers' pain, not to mention the depth of my brothers.

Adam nods. "Anyway, I've told you everything I know. But honestly, Bean, I think you're wasting your time. We should all accept that there was more going on with him than any of us understood. Even you."

I feel like I've been stabbed in the heart by this remark. "You're probably right," I say.

Adam stares off into space. "There was one more thing. It's probably nothing, but right before we headed out, Sam called Skip. He told him that he wouldn't be at his party unless he was able to sneak out after Mom and Dad went to bed, which would probably be very late, given that they were entertaining. I obviously didn't hear Skip's side of the conversation, but from what I did hear, it sounded like Skip was going to come over, because Sam told him to come to his window, not the front door. I figured Skip was dropping off some weed or something."

"Skip was here that night?" I say.

"I don't know for sure, but it definitely sounded like he was coming over."

"But Sam was clean. There were no traces of any drugs in his body."

Adam frowns. "How do you know that?"

"I requested a copy of his autopsy report from the hospital."

He frowns.

"What?" I ask.

"I figured Skip unknowingly gave him some pot that was laced with something that made him delusional or deranged or something. That's the only thing that made any sense to me. And I figured that it also explained why Skip disappeared, because who could handle that level of guilt?"

My mind was racing about Skip and the window and my odd, recurring dream. What did any of it mean? "I just found out about Skip's breakdown," I say. "It's weird, isn't it?"

"It is if what you're saying is true. But they were really tight. Maybe it was too much for him to handle," Adam says, shrugging. "Anyway, if we're done, I should probably go help Dad box shit up." He turns to leave.

"Hey Adam?"

"Yeah?" he says, turning back around.

"You and Chase shouldn't feel bad for not helping him with his paper. It's not your fault that he flaked out and didn't write it."

He shrugs. "The hardest part is that I don't know if he really knew how much I loved and respected him." I see his tears welling up, and I move closer. Before I can hug him, he wraps his arms around me and holds me so tightly to his chest that I actually feel his heart beating.

When he releases me, I look him in the eyes. "He knows, Adam. I know you don't believe in the afterlife and stuff, but I do, and so did Sam, and I promise you that wherever he is right now, he knows you and Chase love him. It doesn't matter that it was left unsaid. It's deeper than that," I say, trying to assure both of us.

"Well, I'd sure like to believe that. I only wish that I were half as sure about the world as you seem to be." He turns and moves toward the door.

"Love you, Adam," I say.

"Love you, too, Bean," he says.

I sit on my bed and reflect on our conversation. How is it that I can assure Adam about the afterlife, but now have doubts about it myself? Sam and I used to talk about how weird it was that we seemed to remember the time between lives, when so few others did. Did someone forgot to cleanse our memory banks? Right now, there are at least ten books on this subject sitting on my bookshelf. Some are stories of mediums who've channeled those who've passed, and others are first-person accounts of near-death experiences or accounts of past-life regressions under hypnosis. The information in all of these cases is nearly identical. Our souls spend the time between lives reflecting on our past life in order to design future lives that will best allow us to continue to grow and expand. Souls are pure vibrational energy so they can't die; they can only transform. It's obviously way more complicated than that, but that's the basic gist. This is something I've always believed from the deepest part of my soul. So, why is it so hard for me to believe that Sam *chose* to leave when he did? Is it because it was so abrupt? Because I often can't feel him around me? Or, because I'm not sure if a suicide is an accepted way to cross over? All I know is that Sam's death is making me doubt my soul-wisdom, and that is the scariest thing of all.

I hear them boxing things up and I decide to go in and offer to help. It's the last thing I want to do, but I'm sure we all feel that way. Dawg is sitting in a new dog bed right outside their door, looking very dejected. I scratch her ears, but she barely acknowledges me. I grab her dog bed with both hands and slide it down the hall and into my room. I leave it next to my bed and then give her a pat on the head. She stares at me, and I think she looks a little less sad than before, though maybe that's just wishful thinking.

"I know I'm not Sam, but I'm going to take care of you from now on. I promise." She looks up at me and then rises and follows me back to the boys' room. Oh well, at least I tried.

When I offer to help, they gladly accept. Dawg continues to follow me back and forth from their room to the attic as I move the last of the boxes. I guess I'm her new master. Either that or she's simply following Sam's scent.

When we finish, Dad suggests we all go relax in the den. After placing our order for Chinese take-out, I leave the room to call Julie. We'd made plans earlier to do something tonight, but I tell her that I want to hang with my family. She's cool with that. When I walk back into the den, Mom's there, sitting on the sofa next to Adam, and they're all talking about Chase's hockey game. I tell her how proud I am of her for going to the game, and she admits that she watched it from the press box, not from the stands.

"That's okay. You're making an effort; that's what really matters," I say.

Chase stands up and gives her a hug. "My game-winning goal was for you, Mom. I saw you up there, and I felt your support. It meant a lot to me to have you there."

The air in the room is much lighter than it's been in a long time. It's been a momentous day for lots of reasons, and I think we're all feeling a slight shift from grief to gratitude. While it's true that Sam is no longer with us, at least not in the physical form, we need to remember how lucky we are to have each other. And hopefully soon, as my faith is restored, I'll be able to reconnect with Sam's spirit, in one way or another.

EIGHT

Sunday morning, I wake up to the smell of bacon. It's been a very long time since I've smelled anything cooking in our kitchen. And even though I'm a vegetarian, I still *love* the smell of bacon. I won't eat it, but I have to admit (sorry, all you pigs out there) that it sure does smell delicious. I get out of bed, make my way to the kitchen, and see my parents at the stove, cooking side by side. Mom has actually showered, and she's not wearing sweats. She's sporting jeans and a pretty baby-blue sweater and maybe, just maybe, she's put on a little blush. They haven't yet noticed me, so I stand there for a moment, taking it all in.

Mom turns around. "Morning, Bean. Could you knock on the boys' door? Adam's leaving soon, and I want us to have breakfast together before he takes off. I've got oatmeal cooking for you."

"Will do, and thanks! Oatmeal sounds great," I say. Dad winks at me. I'm sure he's relieved to have Mom up and about and also to have us behaving like a family again. I feel a weight has lifted off me as well.

Breakfast feels almost normal—the way it did on any weekend morning before Sam passed. We are joking with one another, talking about our summer plans and Adam's classes. Just as we're clearing the dishes, we hear a car horn. It's Adam's ride back to school. He grabs his duffle and hugs our parents goodbye. And then, unexpectedly, he puts his arm on my shoulder, leans closer, and looks me in the eyes. "Let me know what you're up to. Text me or whatever. Maybe next fall you and Julie can come and stay with me for a weekend. I just signed a lease on a cool house with five of my frat brothers. I'm sure I'll have to guard you like a hawk around those guys, but I'd love to show you the campus and the town of Madison. I think you'd really like it there."

I smile. "I'd like that. Thanks. And I promise I'll keep in touch."

When we've finished loading the dishwasher, I go back to my room and rehash what Adam said. Something about guarding me like a hawk. Does he mean what I think he means? That he's worried his roommates will be *attracted to me*? Though we're only five years apart, until now that distance has seemed vast. In fact, he always introduces me as his kid sister, usually while patting the top of my head, like I'm some shaggy puppy dog. But just now, something felt different. Like he was seeing me for the first time not as a little sister, but as a real person. A real person who might even be somewhat attractive. It's been nearly four months since I've seen him, and in that time, I've grown almost two inches, and my body has definitely changed. It's nice that someone's noticed, because besides Richie, whom I've still only spoken to very briefly, most of the time I feel pretty invisible.

My homework complete, I figure it's a good time to tackle the Inuit books to see if they contain anything helpful. I call Julie and ask her to join me. After about twenty minutes reading one of the books, Julie says, "The Inuit basically believe that when people die, they either go to the upper or lower regions. It says, 'These people have an idea of a future state and believe that death is merely a separation of the soul and the material body. The place to which the soul goes depends on the conduct of the person on earth and especially on the manner of death. Those who have died by violence or starvation are supposed to go to the region above. All desire to go to the lower region and afterwards enjoy the pleasure of communicating with the living, which privilege is denied those who go above.'"

Julie looks at me as if she's trying to decide if she should continue. "Go on," I say.

She nods. "'If the death results from natural causes, the spirit is supposed to dwell on the earth after having undergone a probation of four years' rest in the grave. During this time, the grave may be visited and food offered and songs sung, and the offering, consisting of oil and flesh, with tobacco for smoking and chewing, is consumed by the living at the grave.'"

"I don't like that natural causes part," I say. "It's hard to imagine any scenario where his death could be considered natural.

And probation? Makes it sound like the person did something wrong by dying. And what's with the four-year resting period? I can't wait that long. Anyway, it seems crazy that if you die from something you had no control over, like violence or starvation, you'd be punished for it. That makes no sense."

She nods. "I thought so, too, when I first read it, but if you think about it, having such beliefs was probably crucial to their survival. It would have stopped the Inuit from fighting among themselves and encouraged them to share their food when times were tough. They needed to get along because they had to hunt in packs like wolves due to the size of the prey they were going after."

"That makes sense, I guess, and we probably shouldn't take this stuff too literally."

Mostly scientific journals and ethnographic notebooks, the books are tough to read and very dull, but we persist. A few minutes later I find something interesting. "'The *atka* is the soul of a dead person who has been summoned to a child to remain by it and be its companion, protector, or guardian angel.' I might not be a child, but maybe because I'm so incredibly needy, Sam will make an exception."

"There are exceptions to everything," Julie says.

By now we're both on our stomachs with our books propped up in front of our faces. Julie rolls onto her side to face me, propping her head up with her hand. "You're going to like this: 'Spirits are eager to serve them. If they should call the spirits, they would come at once.'"

"Who's *they*?"

"Shamans," she says, smiling.

"Why are you smiling? We aren't shamans, nor do we know anyone who is."

"Maybe we are, and we don't know it." Julie points to my laptop. "Google it."

I jump up and search "shaman" on my computer. "It says, 'It's an umbrella term used by anthropologists to describe a vast collection of practices and beliefs, many of which have to do with divination, spirit communication, and magic.'"

"That sounds pretty broad," Julie says. "I mean, we are into the *idea* of spirit communication, so I guess we could loosely be considered shamans. What do you think? Should we try performing a shamanic ritual to get Sam's attention?"

I move back next to her on the floor. We're both sitting cross-legged facing one another. "I'd be down with that. But how would it work?"

"We'd gather up things that were important to Sam and put them around us and do some sort of ritual. We might not be able to find out what happened that night, but wouldn't it be wonderful if we were somehow able to get real proof that he's around us still?"

"It would. But where and when would we do this?" I ask. "It can't be at his grave. I'm definitely not going anywhere near there."

"How about out at Sam's lean-to on the Enchanted Forest Island? We can sleep out there some night and make an altar with everything that Sam would be drawn to. He would be totally into that. Maybe we could even do it this weekend?"

"It's not even April yet. We'll freeze," I remind her.

Julie shrugs. "Stop being such a wimp. Sam would be so disappointed in you. Who cares how cold it is? We'll make a big fire and add extra blankets. It'll be fun. And it's far enough from your house that your parents won't see our altar. Unless you think you should tell them."

"I don't know what to do. I'm sure Dad would be totally opposed to the idea. Mom would be totally cool with it, and if she was her old self, I'm sure she'd want to be a part of it. But Mom isn't her old self, and I worry that this might somehow set her back. Let me think about how I want to handle it. But wait, will this even work? What if we go to all this trouble and nothing happens?" I ask. I can't seem to get out of my negative headspace even when I'm trying really hard not to let myself go there.

"Bean, you can be such a Debbie Downer. Ever heard of nothing ventured, nothing gained? Besides, what else do we have going on this weekend?"

I think for a minute before answering, but quickly conclude that this is likely one of the last weekends we'll have before the ice becomes too thin to walk on. Then it will be weeks before the ice completely melts, and taking everything over there by boat would be much trickier. Plus, now that we have the idea, I don't want to wait. "Okay, let's do it."

"Great. So, we'll need to start collecting things he really liked in order to appease his soul."

"We'll for sure bring these Inuit books." I stand up and grab the leather-bound "My Journey" notebook to start making a list.

"Yes, and we'll make him a peanut butter and jelly sandwich and add some Skittles, and we can burn some of his incense. You took that from his room, right?"

"I've got it."

"We'll also need some all-purpose good luck charms."

"Like what?" I ask.

"Think your mom would mind if we borrowed some stuff from her Just-In-Case box?"

In many ways, Sam was lucky. He found his Inuit beliefs early on, and they resonated so strongly with him that he never had to look any further. Mom and I haven't been as lucky. We've been on a constant search for something—some belief or religion or whatever—that pulled on our hearts and helped us make sense of this crazy world. We've attended every church in a sixty-mile radius and studied numerous Eastern and Western philosophies together, but nothing has really stuck, besides a general desire to be the best people we can be, and to try and keep our hearts and minds open to what the universe is trying to teach us. Along the way, Mom collected talismans, or charms, or whatever you want to call them, and on her last birthday, in late September, Sam presented her with a super-cool, huge wooden shadowbox he'd built using old barn wood. The back is lined with olive-green velvet that Mom had once made a long evening dress out of, and across the top he arranged twigs to spell out *Just In Case*. Inside, he artistically displayed her feathers, dream catchers, charms, icons, amulets, tree branches, Buddhas, Milagros, crystals, and rocks around a large wooden cross. Mom was completely blown away by it, and I have to admit I was a tad jealous he hadn't built it for me. It hangs prominently in our front hallway so everyone who enters our house can see and appreciate it. Everyone but Dad, that is. I'm sure he feels like we're announcing to the world just how *out there* we are.

"That's a great idea, but I'm not sure we can pull that off. How would we take it out and put it back without anyone noticing?"

Julie shrugs. "I guess you're right, and I don't think it's crucial. We can still find so much other stuff."

"Okay, let's keep reading and see if it explains exactly how we're supposed to do the actual ritual."

After a few minutes, I hear Julie sigh. "What is it?" I ask.

She looks concerned. "There's more stuff here about death. Particularly about suicides."

"Are you shitting me?" I say. "Inuit commit suicide?"

"Bean, there probably isn't a single culture anywhere in the world that's suicide-free."

"Whatever. Just tell me what it says."

"It says suicides 'are not rare. Pitching themselves from a cliff or producing strangulation are the usual methods.'"

"*What?* It actually says *strangulation?*"

Julie nods, but keeps her eyes on the book.

"They think it's perfectly fine to kill themselves by *strangulation?*" I demand.

"Correction. It doesn't say they thought it was okay—just that they did it."

"But Sam made them seem like the happiest and most enlightened people on the planet. Why would they kill themselves?"

"They did it either because they were 'remorseful or because they were disappointed in love.' You said his breakup with Jenny was no big deal. Was there anything else he might have been remorseful about?"

"Maybe killing the deer? But that still makes no sense. Even if he felt remorse, which I'm sure he did even though it clearly wasn't his fault, there's absolutely no way that doe's death would cause him to take his own life," I say, though I can't absolutely guarantee there's no connection. I think again about Skip. He would most likely know if there was something Sam might have been remorseful about, but he's not around to ask.

"Let's get back to our list," she says. "What about Sam's feathers? Did you find them?"

When I tell her Adam has them, she looks as surprised as I was when I heard about their whereabouts. "Are the feathers in their room, or does he have them at school?"

"I have no idea."

"You need to ask him because I think they're really important."

"I'll text him," I say, already dreading the thought. What will I say I need them for?

I feel anxious all week. Every day it gets a little warmer, and the ice gets a little thinner. I've noticed that a few of the heavier rocks that are part of the barrier look like they've begun to sink into the ice. But I check the ice report, and it estimates that it will be safe to skate on the ice for about ten more days. The doe's presence has always felt like a ticking time bomb—like I have to solve the mystery of Sam's death before she falls through the ice *or else*. And I can't imagine that happening because our journey appears to be coming to an end—a dead end. The only person on my list I haven't spoken to besides Skip is the pizza delivery guy, and what are the chances he'll have anything to add? And if this shamanic ritual doesn't work, which is very possible, given our low level of expertise in this area, then I'll never find out how Sam ended up with a belt around his neck or be able to assure myself that he's still with us. Which puts me right back where I was when I started this whole mess.

To make matters worse, Mom still hasn't told Dad that she isn't taking her meds. She said she was going to tell him this week, but then she had a few rough days and decided the 'timing wasn't right.' And I know that if I have to be the one to rat her out, it won't go well. I feel like we're all doing a lot better than we were, but this could be a major setback because Dad has no tolerance for deception. He'll feel horribly betrayed and I can't blame him. Plus, I know they're going to find out about our shamanic ritual. Sleeping outside in March will definitely raise suspicions. Sam was into winter camping, but I wasn't.

On Thursday, Richie sees me standing in the bus line and offers me a ride home. I've been thinking about him a lot, and there's no denying that I have a crush on him, but I feel so unsettled about Sam and about Skip, whose unexplained absence has left a hole in my heart, that it just doesn't feel right to be starting a relationship. But he's sweet and *hot* and I'm not a big fan of buses, so I gratefully leave the bus line.

He's quite the gentleman. He jumps out of his truck, walks around to open the passenger door for me, and then walks back around to the driver's side and gets in. Rather than starting the truck, he sits back and looks over at me. My heart is pounding and my hands are shaking. I move my hands under my legs, hoping he hasn't noticed how nervous I am.

"Is everything alright, Bean?" he asks.

"Yeah, why?" I say, trying to sound normal, though even my awkwardly high pitch is yet another giveaway as to how uncomfortable I feel.

"I don't know. Just get the feeling that you've been avoiding me lately."

I nod. "You might be right." He'd left a couple of notes in my locker asking for my cell number, and I never responded.

"Do you want me to back off?" he asks.

I take a deep breath and look down at my lap. I can't imagine what I could possibly say to him that wouldn't sound totally deranged. "I guess I'm still grieving Sam, and I don't know if it's a good time for me."

"I totally understand, and I don't want to pressure you. If the time isn't right, I'll back off. Not happily, but I will. This must be really hard for you. He was so cool, and way deeper than most people imagined."

"You knew him?" I ask, surprised.

"Freshman year we had lockers next to each other."

"But did you ever hang out?"

He nods. "That fall, my uncle Tony was killed in a car crash. He collided with a moose."

"Oh, God. I didn't know he was your uncle," I say, remembering the newspaper headline and the accompanying photo of a horribly mangled car.

He nods. "He was such a good dude, and we were incredibly tight. He was like my best friend. He taught me to skate, and he coached my hockey team throughout elementary and middle school. When he passed, I was really broken up about it, and Sam totally picked up on that and helped me through it."

I feel a rush of relief. Knowing that he knew Sam in any

meaningful way completely changes things. "What do you mean? How?"

"Open the glove box," he says, pointing. "I want to show you something."

I do, and he sticks his hand in, rummages through a bunch of papers and other crap, and finally pulls out a large, flat stone and places it carefully in my palm. "After my uncle passed, Sam and I started hanging out together during lunch. I guess he could tell that I was totally wigged out and needed someone to talk to. Anyway, he explained that people don't really die, that they just move on from their physical bodies. I didn't really buy into that idea too much, but then one day he handed me that rock." Richie points to my hand. He said that my uncle told him to give it to me. And it totally freaked me out because my uncle and I loved hanging out at his lake house, skipping stones. It was kind of our thing."

I open my palm. "This is totally a skipping rock."

"Right? And I'd never mentioned to Sam that we did that, but somehow, he *knew*. Since I didn't tell him, that only leaves my uncle, because no one else knew about it, not even my parents. That realization kind of changed everything for me. It made me more open to the idea that my uncle might still be here. I'm not completely sold, but there have been times when I'm pretty sure I've felt his presence, and it's been really comforting."

Tears start rolling down my cheeks, and a huge lump forms in my throat.

Richie leans over and wipes my tears with the back of his hand. "Bean, what's wrong? What did I say?"

I shake my head. "Nothing, really. It's just that I used to believe that souls couldn't die, and then Sam passed, and . . . well, nothing makes sense anymore. Sometimes I feel that he's around me, but other times I have real doubts."

Richie gently pulls me toward him. I let myself relax into his chest while I take a few deep breaths to compose myself. I seriously can't believe I'm crying in front of him in the high school parking lot. I'm such a loser. Why can't I keep it together?

After a few minutes, he says, "Can I ask you why you stopped believing, Bean?"

I lift my head off his chest, so I can look him in the eyes and gauge his reaction to what I'm about to say. He has the most sincere, caring face I think I've ever seen. I feel zero judgment from him. Instead, there's just a deep desire to understand me a bit better. "If Sam took his own life—which I don't want to believe, but I can't prove otherwise—then I'm not so sure his soul would be allowed to stick around."

He thinks for a minute and then says, "I think you're wrong. The way Sam explained it to me was that energy cannot be created nor destroyed, it can only change forms. So, I honestly don't think it really matters *how* someone dies."

"Then why can't I feel him?" I'm so desperate that I'm hoping a boy I've talked to less than thirty cumulative minutes in my entire life will convince me that Sam is still here.

"I asked Sam the same thing because it didn't make sense that he could communicate with my uncle, but I couldn't. He told me to start by having conversations with my uncle in my head. It sounded pretty lame, but I would've tried anything at that point. At night, I'd lie in my bed and ask my uncle for advice on shit, the way I used to when he was still alive. At first, I was pretty sure I was making his part of the convo up, but the more I did it, the more I started believing that he really was answering me. This is all still pretty out there for me. In fact, you're the only one I've shared this with, but I figured since Sam was your brother, you'd probably understand. My friends would seriously think I was high if I told them."

I smile. "Your secret's safe with me."

"Good to know." He starts the truck and pulls out of the parking lot.

On the way to my house we move away from serious topics and mostly talk about stupid school stuff. My heart eventually calms down, and by the time we turn onto my street, I'm feeling pretty comfortable. He pulls into my driveway, puts the truck in park, and says, "Are you okay with me now? Can we hang out? Maybe grab dinner or go see a movie or something?"

I smile. "I'd like that, and thanks for the ride and also for sharing what you did about Sam. I'm glad you knew him and I'm going to think about what you said." I push down on the door handle and start to open the door, but he's out his door in no time and standing beside me holding the passenger door open for me. He helps me out of his truck and then moves to hug me. "Bye and thanks again," I say.

He smiles. "It was my pleasure."

For months, I've been carrying around the heavy burden of Sam's death and actually using my physical body to protect my heart from further pain. My shoulders have rounded and slumped, and my chest has become visibly more concave. I've started noticing my old-lady posture in the mirror, and it isn't pretty. But as I leave Richie and walk up the path to our front door, I feel myself opening up, standing more erect, and I can actually visualize my heart chakra expanding. And it's all thanks to Richie. He's helped restore my hope and faith. Solely due to Sam's influence, he went from being a nonbeliever to being a believer. And if he could make that leap, then I'm sure I'll be able to find others. No matter what happens going forward, I know now that I won't be alone.

NINE

On Friday morning, the day before our shamanic ritual, I hear a wolf howling as I'm in the kitchen making myself some tea. Grabbing binoculars from the mudroom bench, I begin to search the vicinity. I finally spot it, once again standing on the shore of the Enchanted Forest Island. It's the same black wolf I've been seeing all winter. Suddenly, he stops howling, turns his head in my direction, and seemingly stares right at me. Given the distance and the fact that I'm on the other side of a large picture window, I seriously doubt he knows I'm watching him. But it sure *feels* like he knows.

"Morning, Sunshine. What're you looking at?" Mom asks as she strolls into the kitchen. Her hair's wet so I know she's showered but her eyes are puffy, like she's been crying.

"Look," I say, pointing. I take off the binoculars and hand them to her. "Out there on the left shore of the island. Do you see it?"

"Is that a wolf? What in God's name is it doing out in broad daylight and so close to our homes? I'd guess it was sick, but it's quite healthy looking, isn't it?" She looks once more before handing the binoculars back to me.

I feel incredibly relieved that she's seeing it because almost every time I've spotted it, I've been alone. The one time Julie was with me, it had disappeared before she could see it. "I've been seeing this same wolf all winter. At least a half-dozen times. I actually think it might be Sam or connected to him in some way. Does that sound crazy?"

"Wolves were his most powerful totem animal. If he had to choose an animal to reincarnate into, it would definitely be a wolf."

"That's what I think. Until you saw it, I wasn't even sure it was real. Because no one else has seen it."

"I bet you didn't know that I was going to have a totem pole made for Sam."

"Really?" I say.

She nods. "When your father and I were in Ontario last summer, we met a very cool, grizzled old man who carved the most beautiful totem poles using a chainsaw. His studio was in a tiny shack on the side of the road. We stopped and watched him carve for a couple of hours. He was a fascinating guy and quite talented. I thought it would make the perfect gift for Sam. He'd spent so much time making me my lovely Just-In-Case box, and I wanted to give him something equally special."

"So, what happened?" As soon as those words slip out of my mouth, I feel horrible. Obviously, I *know* what happened. What

I was really asking was whether the totem pole had ever been carved. But before I can clarify what I mean, Mom's eyes well up. "I'm sorry," I say, "I just wondered if it ever got made."

She wipes her eyes and tucks her hair behind her ears. "No. I wanted to order one on the spot, but the man said I needed to give it careful consideration so that I chose the right animals and put them in the right order on the pole. I knew a wolf had to go at the top and a red-tailed hawk below that, but I wasn't sure what should go next, and I really wanted it to be a surprise. Wild Willy—that was his name—gave me a book that he said would help me figure it out."

"Did it?" I ask.

"I started reading it, and then your father lost a big account, and it wasn't a great time for us to spend money on something like that, so I shelved it and thought I'd revisit it in a year or so. I figured it was something Sam would have forever, so there wasn't any real urgency. But now it makes me sad to think about, because I know Sam would've loved it."

I hug her. "He for sure would've loved it. But I think we should still have one made, whenever we can afford it. It could be our memorial to Sam. We can put it down by the lake or near his lean-to on the island."

Mom nods and smiles. "That's a great idea, Bean. I'll talk to your father about it."

"I'd love to help you figure out the rest of the animals. Do you still have the book?"

When I get home from school, the book *Animal Speak: The Spirited & Magical Powers of Creatures Great & Small* is lying on my bed. I look up *wolf* in the index and dig in. It starts by explaining how wolves are the most misunderstood of all the wild animals and are almost the exact opposite of how they're portrayed, which sounds a lot like Sam. Furthermore, it says they never fight unnecessarily, and they teach you to know who you are and to develop strength, confidence, and surety so that you never have to prove yourself to others. It says those with wolf totems are very expressive with their hands, which is funny because Sam was a master shadow puppeteer. He would tie a sheet across the opening of the lean-to and use his hands to act out elaborate Inuit stories. The book also says, *When wolf shows up, it is time to breathe new life into your rituals. Find a new path, take a new journey, take control of your life. You are the governor of your life. You create and direct it. Do so with harmony and discipline, and then you will know the true spirit of freedom.* I read this part about a dozen times because it feels like it's speaking directly to me. If I'm interpreting it correctly, I believe it's telling me that the shamanic ceremony we're planning is a good idea and, more importantly, it's telling me to believe that Sam is still here and always will be. Or am I reading way too much into it?

I pick up my phone to call Julie, but before I can put in her number, it rings. Of course, it's her.

"I just got off the phone with the pizza guy," she says. "Are you sitting down?"

"Why? What did he say?"

"He totally remembered delivering our pizza that night, and he also remembered seeing someone running away from the far-right side of your house. From his description, it sounded like whoever it was was running away from the boys' room."

"It was dark and sleeting. How could he see anything or anyone?"

"He didn't actually see a person. He saw a flashlight beam bouncing around, and he could tell that whoever was holding it was in a hurry to get away from your house."

"How does he know it was our house? He must have delivered a ton of pizzas that night."

"He remembered your address, and he even described your house. Said he'd delivered loads of pizzas to you guys."

"The boys do order a lot of pizzas from John's."

"He also remembered your house because it was the last delivery he ever made. He was driving his uncle's car, and just before he got to your house, his uncle called and told him that he needed to get the car back to him ASAP because it was being repossessed. Right after he left your house, he skidded off the road and nearly hit a telephone pole. Anyway, the thought of crashing his uncle's car made him panic. He delivered our pizza and then headed home. And that was the end of his pizza delivery career."

"This is crazy. First, Adam tells me that Skip was possibly planning to come over, and he wasn't supposed to use the front door. The delivery guy sees someone running from that side of the house. I've been having a strange recurring dream about the window nearest Sam's bed being open during a storm, and, I don't think I told you this, when I went to the boys' room, that same window had a mangled blind and the curtain was water stained."

"Why would this be important?" she asks.

"I don't know. I just can't imagine what Skip was bringing to Sam that was *so* important that he'd come over in that storm?"

"Agree. It doesn't make any sense," she says.

"It sucks that we can't ask him. If it was him, then he was the last person to see Sam alive." As I say this, I feel a shudder go down my body. *Did Skip have something to do with Sam's death?* I don't want to believe it, but it's getting harder and harder to ignore.

"At the very least, he could tell us what Sam's state of mind was," Julie says.

"It's so frustrating. It feels like we're getting somewhere, but I guess we really aren't unless we can talk to Skip."

"Let's not give up hope yet," Julie says. "Who knows what will happen with our shamanic ritual?"

Instead of going to the movies with Julie and some other friends, I've decided to hang out at home and hopefully get to bed early.

I pull out my journal and look over the list of items we'll need for our ritual. The first item is feathers. I take a deep breath and text Adam.

Hi. Hope everything's good with you. I have a weird question. Are Sam's feathers with you or are they here?

Home

Could I borrow them? Just for the weekend?

They're in the drawer under my bed.

Thanks.

You're weird.

I know.

Next, I gather all the Inuit books and stack them on my desk. I consider going up to the attic to grab my sleeping bag and some blankets, but I don't want my parents to hear me and start asking questions. Then again, who am I kidding? There's absolutely no way that we're going to pull this off without my parents finding out. I have to tell them, and if I don't do it now, I won't be able to sleep tonight. I can hear their voices coming from the den. When I walk in, they're playing Scrabble and watching some old black-and-white movie. This sight makes me very happy. It's what they used to do almost every Friday night—before Sam passed. They both look really content and normal. I don't sense any tension between them. Which must mean that she hasn't told him about the meds. But I don't want to think about that right now.

"Who's winning?" I say, walking into the room.

"Your mother," Dad says, "and I'm not happy about it."

I glance at their board, while trying to think about the best way to say what I need to say. "What does 'numen' mean?" I ask, pointing.

"See, even Bean's never heard the word," Dad says, as if my not knowing it should count for something. "I'll read you the definition since I just challenged her and lost." He puts on his reading glasses and picks up the dictionary, still opened to the appropriate page. "It's a spirit believed by animists to inhabit certain natural phenomena or objects."

I take the book from him and read the definition for myself, not quite believing what I just heard. "How do you know this word?" I ask Mom.

"It weirdly popped into my head. Wasn't even positive it was a word until your father challenged me."

She winks, and I smile back. This is the kind of thing that happened a lot to her and sometimes to me, also. The look she just gave me felt reaffirming, like a connection we had with each other and with other spirits has been reestablished. This seems like as good a time as any to come clean about our sleep-out. "Tomorrow night Julie and I are going to sleep in the lean-to on the island."

Dad's head shoots up and he takes off his reading glasses. "Bean, that's insane. You'll freeze your butts off. Why would you want to do such a thing?" he asks.

"I don't know. Guess I want to feel closer to Sam." While it's true, I'm also using his name because I know Dad won't push me too hard.

"You're crazy, you know that?" He stands up and ruffles my hair. "I'm going to make some hot chocolate. Do either of you want a mug?"

"That sounds absolutely perfect. And while you're out there, could you grab a couple more logs for the fire?" Mom says.

"Will do. And you, Bean?"

"Nothing, thanks."

When he walks out of the room, Mom asks, "What's this all about?"

I knew I could never sneak this past her. "We read in Sam's Inuit books about a ceremony you can perform that might help you communicate with someone who passed. I know it sounds crazy, but we thought it was worth a try."

She nods. "Okay, but are you sure you don't want to wait until it gets a tad warmer? What's the rush?"

"I don't know, but we're just really anxious to do it. I promise we'll use lots of blankets. If we're really uncomfortable, we'll come back inside to sleep."

"May I ask what kind of ceremony this is?"

"It's a shamanic ritual. I know it's a little wacky. I mean, obviously, I get that we aren't shamans, but it sounds pretty cool. It's basically a way to call a spirit to you. We figured it would be an adventure, and what do we really have to lose by trying?"

"Wait here, I'll be right back." Mom leaves the room, and when she returns a few minutes later, she has a book in her hand, which she hands to me. "You might find this helpful."

I stare at the book, trying to remember when I'd last seen it. The title is *Awakening to the Spirit World: The Shamanic Path of Direct Revelation*. "This is from that Mother Earth Retreat you went to years ago, right?"

"I can't believe you remembered the name of that retreat. You couldn't have been more than nine or ten."

"I desperately wanted to go with you, but you wouldn't take me. That's why I remember. I was really mad at you."

"Sorry, but it was for adults only. It was soon after my mom had died. I was desperate to reconnect with her on some level."

"Did it work?"

"One evening some Ojibwe tribe elders visited and performed a very intense dance and drum ceremony, and that night I had very vivid dreams of her. It was intense, I remember that."

I open the book and start reading the inside flap. "This sounds perfect. Like *beyond* perfect. Thanks so much."

She smiles. "I'm glad. Now, why don't you take it out of here before your dad gets back and starts asking more questions. Wouldn't want him to shut you down before you've even gotten started."

"Good idea. Oh, and one more thing. Would it be okay if we borrowed some of the stuff from your Just-In-Case box for our ritual?"

She thinks about my request for a few seconds with a worried look on her face. "Okay, but please be very careful and put everything back exactly as you found it."

"I promise I will." I start to leave and then turn around. Lowering my voice, I ask, "Have you talked to Dad yet? Told him that you aren't taking your meds?"

"Not yet, but I will. Soon."

I want to warn her that she only has three days left, but I quickly think better of it. They seem to be working their way back to each other, and I'm afraid of what will happen when he finds out she's been deceiving him. Part of me wonders if he even needs to know about it, if she really is improving. The experts say that openness and honesty are at the root of all healthy relationships, but maybe there are some exceptions to that rule.

I change into my pj's, hop into bed with the book, and begin reading and writing notes in my journal. Almost from the first page, I'm hooked. I feel like the universe is opening up to me, or maybe I'm the one who's opening up to the universe. I mean, what are the chances that this shamanic "how to" manual would appear the night before our ritual? I want to call Julie, but decide I'll wait until tomorrow because I want to see the look on her face when she sees the book.

The preface says, "Shamanism teaches that there are doorways into other realms of reality where helping spirits reside who can share guidance, insight, and healing not just for ourselves but also for the world in which we live. Shamanism reveals that we are part of Nature and one with all of life. It is understood in the shaman's worlds everything in existence has a spirit and is alive, and that the spiritual aspects of life are interconnected through what is often called the web of life. Since we are a part of Nature, Nature itself becomes a helping spirit that has much to share with us about how to bring our lives back into harmony and balance."

This is exactly what I believed, wholeheartedly, until Sam passed, and the world stopped making sense. But as I read these words now, they resonate deeply, from a place at the center of my soul. And it feels validating to see, from yet another source, what I've always felt in my heart and soul to be true. I haven't even finished the preface, and I feel a sense of relief fall over me. I know that if I can just get back to these beliefs, I'll be okay.

In chapter one, it says, *Shamanism is a form of meditation combined with a focused intention.* That sounds totally doable. I know how to meditate; I used to do it twice daily for twenty minutes until Sam passed, and I can be intensely focused when I need to be.

Farther down the page, it says, *A shaman may help restore power and focus to a person who has experienced a traumatic loss.* Bingo! I shut the book and place it on my bedside table. I don't want to read any more without Julie, and I've read enough to put my mind at ease about us doing this ritual. This is going to work. It has to.

TEN

I wake up on Saturday feeling like a new person. I slept for almost nine hours straight. I don't remember the last time that's happened. I shower, dress, and step into the kitchen to make myself breakfast. There's a note on the kitchen counter that says they've all gone to Chase's away hockey game and won't be home until after lunch. A part of me feels bad that I didn't go with them to support Chase, but I'm also relieved to have the house to myself for a few hours. I can take what I need from the Just-In-Case box without Mom breathing down my neck, because I could tell from her reaction last night that she really would prefer that I not touch it.

In the attic, I gather two sleeping bags and four of our thickest wool blankets. I go to the garage next and gather a couple of large tarps, flashlights, a bucket, and a shovel. As I'm piling this next to the other stuff, Julie calls to let me know she's on her way. Hopefully we'll still have time to take down the Just-In-Case box before Mom gets back. It's so big it really is a two-person job. When I go to the boys' room to collect Sam's feathers, I find Dawg, loyally stationed outside their door, lying on her dog bed. She'd wanted no part of sleeping in my room, so I reluctantly dragged it back down the hall for her. I guess if she couldn't be on Sam's bed, she at least wanted to be guarding their room.

As I approach her, she rolls onto her back. I give her some belly loving before entering their room. I pull open the drawer beneath Adam's bed and stare down at the contents in disbelief. The feathers are perfectly displayed on one of Sam's blue bandanas, all lined up in a single row that goes from one side of the drawer to the other. Along the top he's added a few of Sam's favorite T-shirts, and on top of them is Sam's beloved stuffed puppy dog, Puppy, that he'd slept with since he was born. It literally looks like a shrine to Sam, which I guess it is. I hate to tamper with the display, but I agree with Julie that these feathers are super important. I take a quick photo of it with my phone so I can replace everything exactly as it is, then I carefully remove the bandana with all the feathers, and I also grab Puppy. Surely Sam won't be able to resist Puppy. Maybe if I'm super lucky, I can persuade Dawg to sleep out with us. She would make it a slam dunk!

As I'm leaving their room, Julie's walking down the hall toward me.

"I've got the feathers and Puppy, too," I say, holding them up.

"Puppy! Totally forgot about Puppy."

"I'll put these in my room, and then let's tackle the Just-In-Case box. We don't have to worry because I already told my parents what we're doing."

"I'm actually very relieved," Julie says. "It didn't feel right to do it behind their backs, and we don't need any negative energy around us."

After gathering everything, we carefully place it all in a duffle and leave it near the back door. I look out the window and see the shed. "I'm going to grab Sam's fishing pole and a few lures from the shed. Can you double-check our list to make sure we have everything?"

When I return, Julie says we're missing just one thing.

"What?"

"A photo of Sam," Julie suggests. "I think it's important that our altar has a picture of him as the centerpiece."

Not long after Sam passed, maybe a day or two later, I'd collected every photo of him I could find in my room and around the house and put them all in a box, which I pushed under my bed. I couldn't bear to look at his precious image, and I assumed everyone else felt the same. But it was stupid of me, because in the absence of those photos, all I had was the memory of him hanging by his neck from that belt.

"Bean, what's wrong?" Julie asks, startling me back to reality.

"Sorry, I was zoning out. I packed up all the photos of him. It was just too hard—"

"Totally get that," Julie says. "You don't have to explain. We could use Puppy instead."

"No, you're right. We need a photo of Sam."

Julie follows me to my bedroom, where I get down on my knees and slide a box out from beneath the bed. As soon as I see the top photo—a picture of him lying in a hospital, with his arm and leg in a cast from jumping out of a tree—I erupt into tears.

Julie sits down beside me and wraps her arms around me. "You sure about this, Bean?"

I nod. "It's hard to look at him."

"I know what you mean."

I wipe the tears from my eyes and smile. "You know, it actually feels good to cry, if that makes any sense. I sometimes worry that his death has caused my heart to permanently seize up, because these days I rarely cry. I was worried I'd used up all my tears."

Julie pulls me close and leans on my shoulder. "You're a softy. Always have been and always will be. You'll never run out of tears."

I nod, then peer inside the box. "This is too hard. Why don't you choose one?"

Julie carefully lifts them, one by one. She lingers over one and says, "This very famous, award-winning shot is my favorite." In the photo, Sam's holding a worm. I'd taken the picture last May with my new Canon 35mm camera. I'd wanted a shot of Sam and a fish, but he'd insisted on the worm because, he explained, worms were both undervalued and underrepresented. "Everyone's always showing off the fish they caught," he said, "but have you ever once seen a pic of the worm responsible for snagging the fish?" I admitted I hadn't, and he'd gone on and on about how worms were single-handedly responsible for our survival, explaining how if it weren't for worms, we wouldn't have soil to grow our crops and feed our animals.

Sam and I both liked the photo so much that I'd submitted it to our town newspaper's annual photo contest in the Pet category, which was a stretch, I'll admit. I actually received an honorable mention. On the ribbon they wrote, "We found the worm an especially intriguing subject matter."

In the photo, Sam's wearing a blue bandana tied around his head, as was his look, and his long, blond curls flow loosely beneath it to his shoulders. Framed by the perfectly cloudless day, Sam's penetrating eyes are such a vivid shade of blue they look photoshopped. In his right hand, he's holding a succulent night crawler next to his cheek, and he looks so completely smitten that you'd think it was the love of his life.

The reason I'd asked to take a photo of Sam with a fish was because fishing was his favorite hobby. But his whole theory of fishing changed after the Inuit came into his life. Pre-Inuit, Sam fished purely for sport, competing with his friends to see how many they could catch in a given period of time and not really giving a damn if the fish lived or died in the process. But by fifth or sixth grade, after devouring all the Inuit books he could get his hands on, his fishing experience became more spiritual, with his believing, as the Inuit did, that one should only kill another being if one's survival depended on it. This was when he became strictly a catch-and-release fisherman, using only barbless hooks. For a hobby, he carved beautiful lures out of soap just like the Inuit did out of ivory, but he never fished with them. He considered them talismans, and most of those are now displayed in the Just-In-Case box.

"Remember the first time you and Sam took me fishing?" Julie asks.

I did. Julie, Sam, and I had gone fishing one afternoon near the end of third grade. As we were gathering everything needed from our fishing shed, Julie confessed that she'd only gone fishing once before, with her grandfather, and he'd done most of the work. Before we left, Sam spent a good thirty minutes showing her the nicest way to put a worm on a hook and the least harmful way to remove a hook from a fish's mouth, which wouldn't be too difficult because of the barbless hooks.

We headed out to the lake and, in no time, Julie landed two fish. However, her third fish swallowed the hook very deeply and she couldn't dislodge it. Sam took the fish from her, saw that its gills had been partially ripped out, and said, "She's not going to make it. We've got to put her out of her misery quickly. Do you think you can do that?"

Julie was wide-eyed. I don't think she even understood what he was asking.

Sam bit the top of the fish's head to instantly kill it. Julie nearly fainted watching him. "Grab that water bottle," he instructed, pointing to the bottom of the boat. Julie handed it to him. "No, you keep it. Take the top off and pour some of the water down the fish's throat," he directed as he held out the fish to her. She looked confused but did as she was told. "Is this the first time you've killed a fish?" he asked. She slowly nodded but I could tell she was completely weirded out. "It's important to mingle your blood with this fish's blood so there's no bad blood between you." He took his pocketknife out and handed it to her.

She took it but stared at me as if hoping I'd intervene and stop the madness. When I didn't, she asked, "You're kidding, right?"

"It's not a big deal. Just prick your finger enough to make it bleed and drag it across the wound in its neck. It will help bring your souls closer together."

I look up and nod at Julie. "Yes, I remember that day," I say, laughing. "I thought you would either get it or you'd run away from our family and never return."

"Believe me, the thought crossed my mind," she says. "So, that's what he was doing with the deer we hit that night, right? Mingling his blood with the doe's to appease its soul?"

"Yes."

"Was there something that made that doe's death different?" she asks. "He was so messed up after the accident. I've always wondered."

"I wondered the same thing," I say. "But we've read most of those Inuit books, and as far as I can tell, a soul is a soul; doesn't matter who or what it is, you treat it the same."

Julie looks at the photo once more before placing it in the duffle. "The last two things we need from the house are a peanut butter and jelly sandwich and some Skittles."

"Why don't you go make the PB&J, and I'll search around for the Skittles," I say.

I look in every place I can think of, but I can't find a single Skittle. As I'm looking through the two junk drawers in the kitchen, Mom and Dad walk in. Dad places a sack of groceries on the counter and then turns around and looks at our pile. "I see you girls are really going through with this?"

"We are," I say.

"Well, before you set out, I want to check the ice." He goes back into the garage to grab his auger and then heads down the backyard. Julie and I are staring at each other with bug eyes. We hadn't even considered that the ice might not be thick enough for us to safely walk to the island. Julie and I both cross our fingers.

As Mom is taking off her coat, she asks, "Can I speak to you alone for a moment, Bean?"

"Sure. Julie, I'll be right back."

I follow Mom to the den. "What's up?" I ask, fearing she's having second thoughts about allowing us to go through with this.

"I wanted to let you know that I told your father."

"About not taking your meds?"

"Yes."

I feel a huge sense of relief. I didn't feel any tension between them, so hopefully my fears were unfounded. "How did it go?"

"Honestly, not so well at first. But we sat in the parking lot after the game and talked about it for nearly two hours, and I think he somewhat understands why I did what I did. He agrees that I'm improving. I did pretty well at the game today. I didn't seclude myself. I actually sat with Dad in the stands. Of course, I broke down a few times when I saw old friends who I haven't seen for a while, but I think that's to be expected. Anyway, we agreed that we'd both meet with my psychiatrist next week to tell him and get his blessing, but all in all, it went better than I expected, and it's certainly a huge load off my mind." She wraps her arm around my shoulder. "Thanks for keeping my secret for as long as you did and for trusting me. I know that it wasn't easy. And thanks for pushing me to come clean. As much as I wanted to just move on and not tell him, being honest with him was the right move. With any luck, hopefully tonight, I'll get the first sound sleep I've had in months. But before I do, I promise I'll say a little prayer that you're successful tonight and that you get all the answers you're hoping for."

"Thanks, Mom." I give her a kiss.

"Can I make you girls something for dinner? Your dad wants linguini."

"I'll check with Julie, but I think we might just have Sam's favorite meal.

"PB&J's, potato chips, and cream soda?" Mom asks. I smile, and she adds, "A food connoisseur Sam was not!"

I laugh, then smile. It's the first time since Sam's been gone that we've made light of him. It feels like a new beginning, like a way forward.

I walk back to the kitchen to help Julie make the sandwiches. Just as we're finishing, Dad walks in and starts stamping his snowy boots on the floor mat. "Well, you're in luck, but just barely. It's a little over four inches, so this will likely be the last time you can safely be on the ice until next winter. But stay clear of the black hole where the doe is. I heard a lot of gurgling around there, and the rocks are already starting to sink."

Julie and I high-five each other, though I don't know what to make of the rapidly disappearing doe.

The pile we have by the door is huge. I'm about to suggest that we go out to the island lean-to for the ritual but come back in to sleep, when Dad chimes in.

"I would ask why you need this much stuff just to sleep out for a night, but your mom already told me about your plans for a ritual, so I won't try and talk you out of it, even if I do think it's a bit insane. Anyway, I'm at your service. I think we should get it all down to the shore and then we'll put everything on the tarp and drag it over the ice. Actually, why don't you two bring all this stuff down, and I'll meet you there with some firewood. It doesn't look like you've packed that yet."

"Thanks, Dad. That would be hugely helpful."

"I'll leave the back floodlights on for you in case you want to come back here to sleep. And I'll leave my phone on and have it on the nightstand if you need anything during the night."

"Thanks, that would be great."

It takes us two trips and more than an hour to get everything brought over, dragged to the lean-to, and unloaded. By the time we finish it's nearly 7:00. Sunset is in about thirty minutes, so we'll have to work fast. On the second trip, I used dog treats to lure Dawg out of her bed. I didn't think I stood a chance, but she followed us all the way here and continued following me even after I ran out of treats. She's especially curious about the bag we have with all the trinkets we gathered for our ritual. She keeps sniffing it and pawing at it.

To make the most of the last of our daylight minutes, we decide to divide the work. Julie works inside the lean-to, sweeping out the winter's accumulated debris of mouse droppings and spider webs and then setting up our sleeping bags and blankets. I shovel off the fire pit, start a fire, and then focus on shoveling snow into a large mound to use as our altar.

Together we start to construct the altar. I put Sam's photo in the center, hang Puppy over the top, and then we begin very carefully arranging all the other items in a circle around the photo. When we're finished, we stand up to see how it all looks.

"How totally cool is that?" Julie asks.

I put my arm around her shoulder. "It's a work of art. Who says we're amateur shamans? I guess the only thing missing is the Skittles, but I think that's cool. We have enough other stuff."

Julie pulls out a single yellow Skittle from her front jeans pocket and holds it up to show me.

I gasp. "Where'd that come from?"

"It was divine intervention. I found it wedged between two planks of the lean-to."

"Of course you did! Why don't you place it on Puppy's head. And I don't know about you, but I'm starving. I'll heat up some water for hot chocolate, and then let's eat our sandwiches and chips while we read over that book I was telling you about. I think it will help us come up with a more concrete plan for our ritual."

"Sounds like a plan," Julie says.

By the time we're sitting down in the lean-to eating our sandwiches, the sun has set. I locate my backpack, unzip it, find the shaman book, and hand it to Julie. I also take out my journal. She looks at the cover and frowns. "Your Mom just *happened* to have this book?"

"I know, weird, right? And it totally validates what we're doing. No such thing as coincidences, right? Just co-incidents. The book is basically a how-to manual for shamanic rituals. I wrote down seven basic steps in my journal. Here's what we're supposed to do.

"First, I downloaded an app of Native American drumming, which I'll play when we're ready to begin. Second, I came up with an intention that I think is simple and direct. You're supposed to have the word *need* in it, so I was thinking, '*Sam, I need to know that you're still here. Please show us, in any way you're able, that you are.*'

"In step three we close our eyes and focus on something in nature to act as our portal. Trees are considered guardian spirits, so I think we should use that big pine right there." I point with my flashlight. "It's just a focal point; we don't have to physically go there.

"Step four—after stating our intention, we silently ask for a spirit animal helper. The book said it could be any animal, even mythical creatures. And all animals are equally powerful. So don't be disappointed if a mouse shows up to guide us. In step five, it says when we find our animal, we should build a relationship with it by asking questions for anything we want help with. This could also happen naturally. From there we just watch events unfold and try to learn from them.

"Step six—the ritual will end when we hear a period of rapid drumming. At that point it's important to say goodbye and thank you.

"And finally, the seventh step is this: If we are ready to come back before we hear the rapid drumming, we simply retrace our steps by going back through the tree portal."

I pause and then continue. "The book also said it's important to remember that this is a practice. No judgment or disappointment. Let whatever happens, happen, and if nothing happens, that is cool, too. Does all this make sense?"

"I guess so, but I don't care what it says, I will not appreciate having a mouse as my guide."

I laugh and lean into her, placing my head on her shoulder.

"Before we start, I just want to say I'm feeling incredibly grateful to have you in my life. I'm sure you're the only other person in this town, probably the entire county—if not the entire state— who'd be open to doing something like this with me."

"I'm equally grateful to have you in my life, Bean, and I'm excited to do this with you—even if it turns out to be nothing more than an adventurous winter sleep-out."

ELEVEN

It's a little after 9 p.m., and we're feeling excited and a bit anxious. It's cold but the bucket I filled with melted snow—for putting out the fire in an emergency—is still liquid, so it must be above freezing. The sky is perfectly clear, and it's beginning to sparkle with stars. The moon slowly rises through the branches of the pine trees as we begin our preparations. I grab the tarp and move it outside, nearer to our altar, so we don't have to sit in the snow. Meanwhile, Julie throws a few more logs on the fire, then lights six sticks of Sam's incense and places them in the snow around the perimeter of the altar.

We look at each other and then at the altar. "I know we're mere novices at this, but this looks pretty alluring," Julie says. I laugh and sit down, cross-legged, and Julie sits facing me. I look at Dawg, who's in the lean-to, comfortably burrowed into my sleeping bag. I hate to disturb her, but I think she'd want to be a part of this. She'll make the decision. I pat the ground and gently call her name. She raises her head, dutifully stands, walks over to me, and then lies down beside me, placing her head in my lap. This is more affection than she's shown me in a long time, and I want to believe it means something.

I open my journal and place it on the ground between us. In it we've written passages I thought would be a good starting point. When I open it, Julie nods and closes her eyes.

I begin. "Sam, we need to know that you are still with us. Please help us see you."

We take a few long, deep breaths to settle in. "O, mourn not for the early dead who calmly pass from earth," I read aloud. "The mortal side was laid aside to give the spirit birth."

I turn the notebook around to face Julie, and she reads, "Sam, if you're present, please do not hide. Show us where on this planet you have chosen to reside. Help us broaden our vision and open our hearts, so we'll be forever reassured that we're never far apart."

I activate the drumming app, and we start taking deep, synchronized breaths. As soon as I close my eyes, my thoughts drift farther and farther away from my conscious mind. The drum sounds fade into the background, and the night sounds get louder and clearer. A dog barks far off in the distance, there are footsteps of something very small darting around in the snow, and I hear what I believe is the sound of bat wings, flapping in the sky. My hearing is hypersensitive, probably as keen as a dog's. After a short while I begin to see a dirt path winding through a beautiful forest with tall pines and a floor sprinkled with a diverse array of wildflowers. It's sunny, beautiful, and extremely peaceful: the kind of place you wish you could enter and never leave. I'm making my way along the path, though I can't see my feet or any part of my body. I'm floating along behind a black shadow—or maybe a figure of some kind—that's moving ahead of me, far in the distance. I can't quite make it out. As I get closer, it stops and looks back at me. I see clearly that it's a black wolf, and I understand that I'm meant to follow it.

The wolf lopes down the path, and I float right along behind it. Up ahead, sitting against a large tree trunk, is another figure. When we get up closer, I see that it's Skip. I can't see his face because his head is hanging down, but there's no mistaking his thick auburn hair, which is drawn into a ponytail and hanging just to his shoulders. The wolf sits beside him and begins to lick his face and neck. I sense that Skip is sad or maybe depressed and the wolf is trying to make him feel better. I want to go to him and lend him my support, but I'm frozen in place. I can look around, but I can't move. A voice in my head explains my role is solely as an observer. I may not interact or question what I'm being shown. In my head, I start asking every "need" question I can think of. *Sam, I need to know what this means. I need to know what you are showing me. I need to understand if Skip had something to do with your death. I need you to help me understand why you aren't here and where you've gone.* The wolf stands, turns back around, and starts walking toward me, looking straight into my eyes. When he reaches me, instead of stopping, he walks by me, brushing his coarse coat of fur against my legs. I am profoundly calm for the first time since Sam left. I don't think I actually hear any words, but the message I get, loud and clear, is that I'm going to be alright if I can remember that things are not in my control. I'm reminded that to grow, I must surrender to the unknown.

And then just like that, the scene starts to fade. The rapid drum beat returns and I understand that the session has ended, but I wish it hadn't. I say goodbye and thank you, and then focus on floating back out of the tree trunk portal. All too quickly, I'm back in my body, and it's not at all a good feeling. The weight of Earth settles in around me: I feel chilled, my butt is sore, and my right leg has fallen asleep. I squeeze Julie's hand and slowly open my eyes.

"That was pretty wild," she says, looking around in circles, one way and the other.

"What happened? What did you see?" I ask.

"I had a hard time settling in. I started to think that I was awful for suggesting we do this, that I was setting you up for disappointment. But I opened my eyes, and you were sitting across from me looking peaceful and happy. I closed my eyes again, and almost instantly I was lifted up into the sky. I was a bird of some sort. I could have been an owl or maybe even a dragon. Whatever I was, I was really big, because the shadow I cast was huge. The coolest part was that I was right here, above us. I could see the lean-to, the fire, the altar, and the two of us sitting here. I also saw a feather floating beneath me, zigzagging down to the ground. It was all so wild. I've never experienced anything like it before. Even though I was asking a lot of *need* questions, I never got any concrete answers, or at least not ones that I could interpret. But it sure was a cool view."

"That sounds magical," I say. "And you know how much Sam loved birds? Plus, I remember reading that the Inuit believe feathers are gifts from heaven sent to remind us that we're connected to everything around us, because they're part of the sky and the earth."

Julie's eyes light up. She looks up into the sky. "You've reaffirmed my beliefs, Sam—or whomever," she says. "I will never doubt again. Promise!" She looks back at me. "And what about you? Did you see anything?"

I tell her what I saw.

"Are you positive it was Skip?"

"Positive."

"But you couldn't see his face," Julie says, frowning.

"Trust me, it was him."

"I wonder what it means. When my dog licks me, it either means he wants attention or forgiveness for something bad he's done."

"Right? It once again makes me wonder if Skip played a role in Sam's death. It seemed Sam was maybe trying to show me that he forgives him. But if I'm interpreting this correctly and Skip was somehow involved, I wonder if *I* could forgive him?"

"As hard as it is for us to understand, I don't believe the universe makes mistakes. Everything that happens is part of some bigger plan. It's just so big that we can't really grasp the larger picture. Does all this sound familiar? It should, because that's what you've always told me."

"I know but it's a lot harder to accept when it hits close to home. But I'll keep working on myself. I'll try to re-remember all that stuff I already know."

A gust of wind blows over us, and the fire roars as if it's applauding. The air suddenly feels charged.

"I'm cold," I say. "Are you ready to get into our sleeping bags?"

"Sure, but do you think we should pack up the stuff from the altar first?" Julie says.

"No, let's leave it. Sam should have at least one night to appreciate it."

"But what if that wolf shows up? I know wolves don't hurt people, but I'm not sure I really want one hanging around while I'm trying to sleep."

"We'll be fine. You know how fearful wolves are of us. If it's still around here, which is highly unlikely, I'm sure it'll keep its distance. And if that wolf is Sam, maybe something magical will happen tonight. In either case, we'll be fine."

"Okay, I trust you," Julie says.

I stoke the fire and then we both bury ourselves deeply into our sleeping bags and pile the extra blankets on top of us. Dawg is in between us, under the blankets, near our feet. We're both silent for about twenty minutes. I like that we are so comfortable with each other that we can stay in silence. I'm not tired, but there's a lot swirling around in my head that I'm trying to process. Finally, I ask Julie, "What are you thinking?"

"I was remembering all the times we slept out here with Sam. I loved hearing his Inuit stories and watching him use his hands to act them out. His stories had such good lessons."

"He was a great teacher," I say. "I admit that I sometimes found his stories pretty annoying, but I can clearly see that teaching was his main role in this lifetime. I wish he was still here because I miss him, and I'm sure I have way more to learn, but I guess in the time he was here, he made a big impact on those of us who were listening."

"I'm so glad I knew him for as long as I did. He was one of the most special souls I've ever known. He definitely taught me a lot and made me look at the world differently."

"For sure. Oh," I say as I roll over to my side and prop my head up on my hand so that I can look at Julie, "that reminds me of something. Richie *knew* Sam."

"Everyone knew Sam," Julie says.

"No, I mean they had a *real* relationship."

"How do you know? When did you talk to Richie?"

I tell her the story of Richie's uncle and the skipping stone.

"Bean, that is incredible. How did you not tell me this before?"

"Honestly, I think I'm still processing it."

"You told me that you couldn't imagine being with anyone who hadn't known Sam, and then you find out that Richie knew him. What are the chances?"

I nod and smile. "I know, it's pretty cool."

"Did you kiss?" Julie asks.

"Seriously? Do you honestly think that if I had, I'd wait three days to tell you?"

"Just checking," Julie says. "Anyway, I can't keep my eyes open much longer. Think I'm going to crash."

"Me, too. I'm completely wiped. It said in the book that shamans often sleep for days after their rituals."

"That sounds about right."

"Goodnight and sweet dreams," I say, pulling my hat down over my ears.

"Night, Bean."

I wake up just as the first rays of sun reach between the pine branches and land on my face. I check my phone and see that it's a few minutes after seven, which means we slept for over eight hours, and yet I still feel a bit out of it. I'm remembering now that I had an agitated sleep. Strange dreams plus I was really cold. I had to pee all night, but I didn't want to leave the warmth of my sleeping bag. I finally forced myself to get up right before daybreak, then had a hard time falling back asleep. I reach over and nudge Julie on the shoulder.

"Jules, I'm sorry to wake you, but I'm really chilled. Want to go inside with me to get warm? We can clean all this up later."

She rubs the sleep from her eyes. "Sure," she says. We slither out of our bags, put on our boots, and wrap the blankets around us. Dawg wakes up, slithers out, and joins us, her tail wagging.

The fire still has red embers. "Did you add more logs?" I ask.

"It wasn't me, but Bean, look," Julie says, pointing to the altar. "The Skittle and the food are missing. Do you think . . . ?"

I look around to see if I can find any tracks, but we've completely trampled the surrounding area. "Could have been a chipmunk or even a squirrel, but I'm choosing to believe Sam was here, in one form or another."

In the kitchen, Mom's sitting at the table having tea and reading the newspaper. "Well, how was it, girls?" she asks.

"It was really cool, but definitely frigid. We need some hot tea, pronto."

"Look forward to hearing all about it," she says. "I'm making popovers. You girls want some?"

"Sure," we say in unison.

Dad walks in the room. "Looks like our winter campers survived. Did you stay out there all night?"

"We did," I say, feeling somewhat proud.

"I went out about 11:30 p.m. or so to check on you, and you were both sound asleep."

"Thanks. And thanks for adding logs to our fire."

"I didn't touch the fire. It was still burning pretty good, and you both looked real cozy under your sleeping bags and blankets. And honestly, I didn't think there was a chance you'd stay out there all night."

Chase walks in a few minutes later and plops down beside me at the table. "I thought I smelled popovers. Thanks, Mom. You definitely know how to get me out of bed." He looks over at me with a confused look on his face. "So, Bean, why the heck did you two sleep outside when it's still frickin' freezing out? And what was all that stuff you piled out there for?"

"How did you even know where we were?" I ask.

"I could see the flicker of the fire through my bedroom window, so I went to check it out."

"Oh, well, we were just practicing this ritual we read about," I explain.

He frowns. "You knew about this?" he asks our parents. "They could have frozen to death out there and probably would have if I hadn't kept adding logs to their fire."

"It was you!" I say, glancing at Julie and feeling a bit bummed. I know we both hoped maybe Sam had had something to do with it. On the other hand, Chase actually walked all the way to the island, more than once, to make sure we were okay, which is super cool and highly unexpected.

"That was really sweet, Chase," I say. "Thank you. I'm surprised you didn't wake us up and make us come inside."

"I thought about it, but then I saw all that stuff, that shrine or whatever, and decided I shouldn't mess with whatever it was you were up to."

After showering, we head outside to start cleaning up. It's a beautiful day, the first really warm one we've had in over six months. The warmth of the sun feels glorious. After our first load, Julie asks if I want to take a minute to sit at the picnic table and soak up some much-needed vitamin D.

"Definitely!"

"This feels great, doesn't it?" she asks.

"Sure does. I'm totally ready to put this bleak winter behind us."

It takes us almost an hour to get everything back to the house. We're just sorting the last of our pile when Julie asks if she can take a break to jump in the shower.

"I'm feeling gross, and I'm still a little chilled," she explains.

"Sure, we're almost finished. I'm just going to put these back in the fishing shed," I say, grabbing Sam's flies and fishing pole.

Our fishing shed is located at the bottom of our backyard, to the right of our dock and close to the shore. I pull open the shed door partway and step inside, and I'm instantly hit with the familiarity of the smells: dirt, rust, lake, and worms, which I hadn't appreciated yesterday in my haste to collect everything. This place is all Sam; he designed it, built it, and spent an extraordinary amount of time in it tying flies and maintaining his fishing rods. Its familiarity makes me feel both sad and nostalgic. The main light over the workbench is out, and the light that does work is very dim, so it takes my eyes a while to adjust. Suddenly, goosebumps appear all over my arms. My heart starts beating loud and clear: *THUMP THUMP THUMP THUMP*. I push the door farther open, and that's when I see him, clear as day. He's sitting on a stool at the bench across the room, wearing a ripped and dirt-stained white T-shirt and jeans, diligently tying a fly. He turns around and looks at me with his impossibly endearing smile, the smile I promised myself I'd never forget, with dimples on either cheek, and with the right side curved slightly higher than the left. I want to run to him, but I can't move. After only a few brief seconds, Sam looks back down and continues working on his fly under the magnifying glass he'd set up. My body releases, and I walk toward him, but as I do, he quickly fades away, evaporating back into the walls of the shed like steam from a kettle. I frantically look everywhere, but he's nowhere to be seen. And yet, I feel him and even smell him. It's both comforting and disconcerting. I take some deep breaths to try and slow my heart. You'd think seeing a ghost would be freaky or at least unsettling, but it was nothing like that. It was incredibly comforting; that's the best way I can describe it.

I replace his pole and flies, turn out the light, and secure the door. I lean with my back against it and try to process what I have just experienced. A few minutes later I hear Dad's voice.

"Bean, are you out here?"

I move around the corner of the shed. "I'm over here, Dad."

He's walking down the hill toward me. "I wanted to let you know that you were right."

"About what?" I ask, confused.

"Look," he says, pointing at the spot in the lake where the doe and barrier used to be, which is now just a large hole in the ice.

My heart sinks. "What happened to it? Where did it go? She was there last night."

"It all sank during the night. You know this spot; it always melts first. Bean, are you okay? You look a little shaken up."

"I'm okay," I say. I do feel strange, but not as bad as I imagined I might feel.

"I know you felt a connection to her, and I know why."

"What do you mean?" I ask.

"When I was walking back from the island last night, I noticed that the ice around her was starting to break up. The rocks had all sunk, but I quickly started grabbing all the wood so a boater wouldn't hit it this summer. When I came back for the last pieces, the doe had become dislodged and she was floating on her side. I could clearly see then that her belly was real torn up. A few minutes later she was gone. Swallowed up by the lake and finally laid to rest."

I can't quite believe what he's telling me. I don't know what is more shocking, the fact that I was right or that my dad took me seriously.

"I don't know how you could have known such a thing," Dad says, "but it makes me think I should listen a bit more closely to what you have to say."

I look at him and smile; he comes over, wraps his arm around my shoulder, and pulls me into him. This level of affection is rare for us but I'm totally digging it. I look up at him and smile.

"Are you going to be okay, Bean?" he asks.

I nod. "I think we're all going to be okay, Dad."

"I think you're right, Bean."

TWELVE

Going to Itasca State Park has been a dream of mine for a long time. I first heard about it when I accompanied Mom to her friend's wedding in New Orleans. While there, we went on a riverboat cruise along the Mississippi, and Mom mentioned that the source of the river was in Minnesota, not too far from our house. From that moment on, I've longed to visit the spot where this mighty river begins its trek, which may also have something to do with how much I love *The Adventures of Huck Finn*. For years, Sam had been promising to take me, because the rest of our family doesn't equate camping with a vacation. But it seemed every time we had a date picked, something would come up, and we'd have to cancel. But now it's finally happening. Julie and I are leaving in the morning.

It will take us about three hours to get to the park, and we'll be there for five glorious days. I'm sitting in my room packing and grinning from ear to ear when the doorbell rings. I almost don't answer it, believing it's either a Jehovah's Witness or someone trying to sell us something. Then Dawg, who rarely rouses herself for anyone, starts barking like crazy. Since she doesn't bark at strangers, like a normal dog, it means she knows the person on the other side of the door. Begrudgingly, I walk into the living room, open the front door, and find Skip standing on our porch. Dawg is ecstatic, jumping nearly vertical into the air, but I nearly collapse from the shock of seeing him after all this time. I literally have to brace myself against the door frame to stay upright.

There has been absolutely no communication between us since Sam passed, which feels way longer than the nineteen months that it's been. If Skip was handsome before, he's drop-dead gorgeous now. That's my first thought, and my second is *Where the fuck have you been all this time, and why have you never contacted me?* But not a single syllable emerges from my mouth. I just can't seem to make sense of him being here; it almost feels like he's an apparition, that I'm only imagining his presence. But Dawg obviously sees him, so he must real.

"Bean, are you okay?" he asks, frowning with concern.

I nod but remain silent. I don't know what reaction he expected, but I can tell that I'm making him feel extremely uncomfortable because he's shifting his weight from one foot to the other, and he's fidgeting with the black baseball cap in his hand.

"May I come in?" he finally asks. I realize then that I've made no attempt to open the screen door.

I push it open and move to the side to let him walk by. His shoulder lightly brushes against me as he passes, and I feel an electrical tingling sensation, which jolts me from my stupor.

Once inside, he steps toward me and wraps his arms around me. At first this feels really good, but then my rage explodes, and I pull free. If he thinks he can waltz back into our lives like nothing happened, he's got another thing coming. In my mind, he's been dead. That's the only plausible explanation I could think of for why he's never called, texted, or even written. "Bean, what's wrong?" he asks.

"What's wrong? Are you for real? What's wrong is that Sam died, and you disappeared. How could you? I mean, I heard you were messed up and all, but seriously? You couldn't have reached out to me even *once* in the last nineteen months?"

"I'm really sorry, Bean. I didn't think you'd want me to. I was waiting for you or anyone in your family to reach out to me, to tell me you forgive me," he says.

"What are you even talking about? Forgive you for what?"

He steps back with a horrified look on his face, and whispers, "For Sam's death."

My heart starts pounding as I try to make sense of what he's saying. "What do you mean? What are you saying?"

"You got my letter, right?" Skip asks.

"No. We haven't received anything from you."

He covers his mouth with his hand and takes a deep breath as tears roll down his face. "Can we sit down?" he asks. "Please?"

We move deeper into the living room and sit on one of the sofas. He sits close to me, but I slide away. "I sent you all a letter to explain what happened to Sam, and in it I asked for your forgiveness. When you didn't reply, I figured you hated me, and I honestly couldn't blame you. But I've always felt cowardly for not coming here to face you in person, so that's why I'm here now."

"I'm sorry, back up. Are you telling me you're somehow responsible for Sam's death?"

He nods slowly.

"*You* hung him?"

"Oh, God, no, nothing like that. It was just so stupid. Let me try to explain," he says, taking a deep breath. "Sam called me that night to tell me he was grounded. He was really pissed off. I don't think I'd ever heard him so angry. To cheer him up, I told him about this crazy shit my stupid cousins in Canada were doing. It's called AEA. They'd sent me the army belt and the instructions. Sam didn't believe me, so I went over to your house right before my party started and gave him it to him—the belt, the instructions, everything. I never imagined, not even for a second, that Sam would actually try it. I was only trying to entertain him, make him laugh. You have to believe me."

"I still don't know what the hell you're talking about, Skip. What's AEA?"

He looks at his feet. "It's autoerotic asphyxiation," he mumbles.

"Still have no clue what that is."

He looks out the window, then back at me. He seems deeply embarrassed. "Basically, the idea is you cut off your circulation while you're masturbating, and it makes your orgasm last longer. But you're never supposed to do it alone. It said that in capital letters at the bottom of the paper. You're always supposed to have someone with you so they can undo the belt or whatever you use. I figured someone must have found the instructions in his room, but guessed that you kept it to yourselves because, you know, it's, well, it's—"

"They found a burnt paper in his wastebasket and I knew that belt wasn't his," I say weakly, "but we had no idea what happened."

Skip's body slackens, and he lets his torso fall back against the sofa. Then he leans forward and holds his head in his hands. When he looks up, his eyes are puffy and red. "I'm so sorry, Bean. I thought you knew. I didn't physically put the belt around his neck, but I may as well have."

"But wait. Something doesn't add up, because when we found him, he was fully clothed, so he couldn't have been doing that."

"You can also do it just to get high. It said that in the paper. I had offered to bring him some pot that night, but he didn't want any because he had to be straight so he could write his paper. I don't know, maybe he thought he could just use the belt for a quick high."

I look over at him, still trying to connect the dots. "So, what you're saying is that Sam didn't want to die? He was just trying to get *high*?"

"Oh, God, is that what you all thought?" Skip starts shaking his head. "No. Shit. No, he'd never kill himself."

"None of us wanted to believe that, but what were we supposed to think? It's what everyone thought—the detective, the coroner, everyone. How could you not know that?"

"I was gone, Bean. By the next afternoon, I was already in a hospital. I was having seriously dark thoughts, and my parents were scared. Two days later I was released and was sent to a treatment center. I had a really great therapist there, and she helped me write you all a letter to apologize and ask for your forgiveness. Afterwards, when no one reached out, I figured you couldn't forgive me, which was totally understandable. I thought the best thing I could do was to stay away and pray that maybe if enough time went by, you'd eventually be able to forgive me."

I frown. "But we never got your letter," I say, still not totally convinced he ever wrote one.

"Are you sure? That doesn't make any sense," Skip says.

Suddenly, I flash back to the basket of condolence cards that I'd stashed in the closet. "Wait here," I instruct. I run down the hall, open the hall closet, take the basket down from the top shelf, bring it back to the living room, and place it on the coffee table. I push it over to Skip. "See if you can find it in here." A few seconds later, he pulls it out and hands it to me.

The letter, addressed to all of us and written on blue stationery, is still sealed. I rip it open:

Dear Mr. and Mrs. Hanes, Bean, Chase, and Adam,

I honestly don't know where to begin, but I have to get these words out, so I'll just start. On the night Sam died, I brought him that paper about AEA, which I imagine you found in his room, along with an army belt. AEA, as you must know by now, is this really stupid game my wacky cousins in Canada are into. Sam seemed really upset about being grounded and I thought he'd get a kick out of it, because we were always laughing about the idiotic things these cousins did. Anyway, that night I went to your house and asked if he wanted any pot, but he turned me down because he had to write that paper, and he knew he couldn't do it stoned. So, instead of pot, I gave him the paper about AEA and the belt. I just did it to make him laugh. I never thought for a single second that Sam would actually try it. But I guess I didn't factor in how upset he was and how badly he wanted to escape that night. I guess he figured this type of high would be over quickly.

All I know is that he never intended to harm himself, and he certainly did not intend to kill himself. I know that for a fact because he told me he'd sneak out and come to my party as soon as you were all asleep, plus, we were planning on taking a big hike on Sunday to Three Lake Falls with two super-hot girls from Rigby High, and we were both psyched about it. He loved life like no one I've ever known. But you all know that better than me. I guess he was just frustrated and wanted to get a little high and then wasn't able to release the belt.

This is a horrible letter to have to write to a family, telling them that I'm responsible for their son's death. I'll leave it up to you to decide if you want to share this information with the police, and I'm prepared for whatever legal repercussions I may have to face. My one and only hope is that someday you will find it in your hearts to forgive me. You were always like a second family to me, and I would hate to lose you, but I'll let you decide if you want me in your life or not. I wish I knew what more I could say to ease your pain, but I really don't. He was more like a brother than a best friend, and I feel truly devastated and lost to be on this planet without him.

When I learned how he died, I couldn't deal. I wanted to die, too, and when my parents found a note I was writing, they immediately took me to a hospital and later to an in-house treatment center. I don't know how long I'll be here, but it's against the rules to make calls or send emails. Should you wish to contact me, you may write me c/o:

Wilderness Center Lodge
55 Oak Street
Grand Rapids, Minnesota 55730
Again, I'm sorry from the bottom of my heart. I love you all and always will, no matter what you decide to do.

Love, Skip

As I read, tears run down my face and the hard lump that has been lodged in my heart all these months actually begins to soften. I reach my arms around Skip and hug him tightly to me. His body collapses into mine, and I feel him trembling. When I release him a few minutes later, he moves just a few inches back and looks me in the face.

With a shaky voice, he asks, "Will you ever be able to forgive me, or is that too much to ask?"

I nod and smile.

A few months ago, I wouldn't have been able to answer Skip with such surety. But something pretty miraculous has happened to my family just in the last year or so. Last April, when my parents went to see my mom's psychiatrist about her not wanting to take her meds, my dad was adamant that she should take them for at least a year. Mom disagreed, and their compromise was that she'd find a new doctor or therapist that they both respected. Through referrals, Mom finally found a faith healer named Mary Starr. Dad was skeptical at first, but over time he loosened up to her ideas, and after a month or so, I could tell that he actually began to look forward to their sessions.

From the outside, it looked like Mom was depressed and Dad was fine, as he appeared to be functioning the way he always did, full steam ahead. But on the inside, I guess it was a different story. Mom was struggling, for sure, but she was allowing herself to go into the pain, while Dad was pushing it down and not allowing himself to feel much of anything. With Mary's help and guidance, they both found their way back to life and, thankfully, also to each other.

Mary suggested books about life after death, and they discussed these books each week when they met. Mom began sending some of the books to Chase and Adam, who were both away at college, and when they came home on school breaks, they individually went to see Mary. I read the books on my own and discussed them with Mom from time to time, but for us it was mostly relearning what we'd long believed yet had chosen to forget when faced with the pain of Sam's death, which was that Sam was here for the time he was supposed to be here and not a moment shorter or longer. We know it will probably never make sense to us on this earthly plane, but we accept it in a more universal way. And though he's no longer with us in the same physical form that he was, I do believe he's never far from me in whatever spiritual form he chooses to take. This is what I believe about the life of all souls.

Now, I know just how to answer Skip. "I already have," I say.

His whole body perks up. "Really?"

"Yes."

"Bean, you can't know how relieved I am. Thank you. Thank you so much."

I squeeze his hand and smile at him. He pulls me in close and gives me a big hug. "When do you think the rest of your family will be home? I'd love to get this over with as soon as possible."

No sooner are the words out of his mouth when we hear my parents coming into the kitchen from the garage.

"Wait here. I'll go get them," I say.

When I return, Skip stands, and my parents rush over and hug him. Skip looks at me, startled. "I didn't tell them any-thing," I explain.

He asks them both to sit down, and then he tells them everything, pretty much the same way he told me. They are both quiet as they struggle to take in this new information. I hand Mom the letter, and she and Dad read it together silently. Dad is the first to speak.

"I can only imagine how hard this was for you to come here today, and I'm very sorry for the misunderstanding. The number of letters and condolence cards arriving daily was overwhelming, and I guess none of us had much interest in reading them. But, son, please know that none of us hold you responsible for the poor choice Sam made that night. That was his own doing. We know you loved him and miss him just as much as we do." Dad pats him gently on the shoulder. "I think it's best if we all just move forward from here. Don't you agree?" he asks, turning to Mom.

She moves over to hug Skip again, and when she releases him, she takes his hands in hers. "Yes, I agree with every word. We've all moved on and we hope you'll be able to, also. I can't imagine the heavy burden this must have been to carry around with you all these months, believing we knew but hadn't been able to forgive you, which couldn't be further from the truth. It's so good to see you, Skip, and to have you in our home again. We've missed you terribly."

"Thank you so much. I didn't really know what to expect, but this is way better than I'd dared hope for," Skip says.

"You're always welcome in this family. And if you have no plans for dinner, we'd love to have you stay and eat the trout we just caught," Mom says.

Skip looks at me to get my blessing, and I smile. "Sure. That would be great," Skip says.

Mom asks where he's staying as she leads us all into the kitchen.

Skip turns around and points to his duffle lying beside the front door, which I hadn't noticed before. "I caught the first flight I could after my graduation and then hitchhiked up here from Minneapolis. I didn't really think it through or even call anyone to tell them I was coming."

"Great, then you'll stay with us for however long you want," Mom says. "The boys are home for the summer, so I can only offer you the den, but I believe you and our big, lumpy sofa are already well acquainted. Why don't you toss your duffle in there and meet us in the kitchen? Bean, can you also lend me a hand?"

"Sure, I'll be there in a minute. Just want to finish packing."

When I walk back into the kitchen a few minutes later, I see Skip and Dad outside, gutting the trout by the trash can and laughing. It truly warms my heart to see this. Of course, I wish it was Sam outside with Dad, but Skip is the next best thing. Mom wraps her arm around my shoulder and follows my gaze outside. "You've still got it bad for him, don't you?" she asks.

"What are you talking about? He's like a brother to me."

"Bean, you're not fooling me for a second. You've been in love with that boy since you first laid eyes on him."

"Well, he is pretty hot! And I'm happy that he's here and that we finally know what happened. I should never have doubted my gut."

"Agree."

I help Mom prepare a salad while Skip and Dad finish gutting the fish and move on to shucking the corn. A few minutes later, the garage door opens and the boys walk into the kitchen. Mom nods toward the window, and they both look outside. "Is that Skip?" Adam asks. "What the hell?"

"Yes, he's got something he'd like to tell you both. Why don't you go on outside?" Mom suggests.

A few minutes later, Mom hands me plates and silverware and asks me to set the picnic table. I walk outside and see Adam and Chase down near the dock, next to our new totem pole, talking to Skip. I can tell from their body language and laughter that they have no problem whatsoever with what he's told them.

We all have a nice dinner together, which feels way more comfortable than I'd imagined it would. I know that we all miss Sam and wish he were with us, but we're going to be okay. I know that now, without any reservations.

After dinner, everyone helps clear and clean the dishes, and then Skip asks if I'd like to go for a sunset cruise with him in our canoe.

I agree but make him thoroughly clean it out because it's full of cobwebs and dirt—none of us has had the heart to use it since Sam passed. When he's finished, he whistles for me, and I walk out on the dock. Skip reaches up to take my hand. I sit on a bench across from him. Once I'm settled in and we've pushed ourselves off the dock, I say, "So, start at the beginning, or maybe start after you left Wilderness, and tell me what you've been up to. Did you really attend a boarding school?"

"Yeah, I attended Chasten in Connecticut."

"Fancy, schmancy. Did you like it?"

"It's very preppy and academic, which isn't really my thing, but it was okay. My dad's brother, my uncle Ted, is headmaster there, and they all thought it would be a good place for me because three of my cousins were already there. I didn't really know where else to go. My parents moved to North Carolina while I was still at Wilderness, so I couldn't come back here. I guess if Sam were alive, I would've asked your parents if I could stay with you to finish my senior year, but since that wasn't an option, I figured a boarding school would be a better idea than starting at a new school in North Carolina where I knew no one. But I've really missed this town and especially this lake. I've always felt I belonged here, but being here now, without Sam, is way harder than I would've imagined."

"I know, that's why none of us have had the heart to get in this boat. But we have to make the most of life. That's what Sam would want for us."

"You're right. You were always really wise for your age," he says, smiling.

I'm praying that he doesn't notice that I'm blushing. "Did you make a lot of friends at boarding school?"

"No, not really. I only went for senior year, and by then most of the guys were pretty tight with each other, and I barely knew my cousins who were there. Then again, it's probably at least partially my fault. I was still pretty messed up when I arrived, and

I can't honestly say that I made much of an effort. I mostly just did the work and kept my head down. It was something to get through, not necessarily enjoy."

"Are you going to college in the fall?" I ask.

"Yeah, I'm going to CU Boulder. I'm actually going straight there from here. One of my favorite teachers at Chasten moved his family to the area, and he invited me to spend the summer with them. I'm helping him build an addition to their house. He's promised to teach me to river kayak and rock climb and stuff. I'm pretty psyched about it, which is good because I haven't felt psyched about anything in a long time."

I want to be happy for him, but honestly, I'm disappointed that he's not sticking around longer. "You can stay with us as long as you want, you know."

"Thanks, Bean. I appreciate that, but I promised I'd be out there before the end of June because the building season is short, like it is here. Tomorrow I'm going to attend what would have been my class's graduation. That's another reason I flew back here. I want to reconnect with everyone before they split for college. I feel bad that I left with no explanation. Pretty shitty of me, actually."

"I'm sure they'll all understand."

Skip nods. "Would you come to graduation with me? I'd feel way less awkward and you know pretty much everyone in our class."

"Sorry, but I can't. Julie and I are heading to Itasca tomorrow morning to camp for a few days before our summer jobs start."

"Shit. So, I won't see you again before I leave?" Skip asks.

"How long are you staying?" I ask.

"I'll be out of here by Wednesday mid-morning."

"I guess this is it, then, because I'm not coming back till Thursday afternoon," I say, trying to hold back my tears. I consider calling Julie and explaining the situation, and calling off our trip; but even though I'm sure she'd be okay with it, it wouldn't be right. We've been planning this for too long. Realizing that this is the last conversation we'll have for a while, I suddenly feel more brazen. "So, do you have a girlfriend?" I ask.

Skip smiles. "No. I'm still waiting for you."

I laugh as if he's joking, but I wish he wasn't; I hope he wasn't.

"And you, Bean? Any guys in your life?"

It feels both strange and completely comfortable to be having this conversation with him. Though it's only been nineteen months since we've seen each other, in that time I feel like I've gone from an awkward teen to a seasoned adult. I guess a loss like the one we've all suffered will do that to you. "Actually, yes. For the last year or so I've been dating Richie Branson," I say. Skip's head shoots up at this news, and I want to believe that he feels jealous.

"He's a good guy," Skip says, "but he's way too old for you. I hope he's being respectful?"

I laugh again. "Yes, very, but we recently broke up. He's heading to McGill in the fall, and I'm stuck here for two more years, so it didn't make sense to have a long-distance relationship. It was never anything serious, but he's a great guy."

"I'm happy for you. You know, the first thing I thought when I saw you at the door was that you'd really changed."

"Yeah, I've actually grown almost four inches in the last year or so."

"You're taller, but you're also just *different*. I always thought of you as Sam's little sister, but you're all grown up now."

My face gets hot and I have no idea how to respond.

"I'm sorry if I embarrassed you. I didn't mean to," Skip says.

I smile. "It's okay."

"Thanks for coming out here with me tonight. Seeing your family and getting everything off my chest feels amazing. I was worried that it was too late, that I'd really blown it, and you wouldn't want me in your lives anymore. But it seems like we're all cool now. Am I right?"

"Totally. Seeing you is really good for all of us. I know you're not Sam, but you're the closest thing we have to him now."

"Thanks, but that's a lot to live up to. "

"So, this is probably a weird question, and it has absolutely no segue, but I'm just wondering *how* you got the bag with the belt to Sam?"

"What do you mean *how*?"

"What door did you use?"

"I didn't use a door. Sam asked me to come to his window so your parents wouldn't see me."

"Which window?"

Skip gives me a bewildering look. "The one closest to his bed. Why?"

"I've been having a recurring dream about that window. I figured it was important, I just couldn't figure out why."

He gives me a funny look. "Only you, Bean. We actually messed up that window pretty bad that night. It was frozen shut because of that ice storm, and Sam was having a really hard time getting it open and he ended up mangling the blinds in the process. Then the curtains were blowing around inside like crazy. We thought it was hilarious, like something out of *The Wizard of Oz*. In fact, Sam's last words to me were him quoting that US Postal Service saying: 'Neither snow nor rain nor heat nor gloom . . .'"

"That's exactly what I saw in my dreams. Not you or Sam, just the mangled blinds and the curtains blowing in."

Skip rows us around the island, and we enjoy a very comfortable silence. It's a magical evening. The sun is slowly setting, and lightning bugs are beginning to twinkle in the sky. "I've missed this so much. This lake is in my blood, and it always will be," Skip says.

I nod. "Yeah, it's pretty great. I'd forgotten how tranquil and special it is. Since Sam passed, we've hardly ventured out on the lake. Last summer I don't think any of us even fished or put our toes in the water. I guess we all connected the lake to Sam and we've been reluctant to enjoy it without him. Now that I'm saying this out loud, it sounds ridiculous, because of course, Sam would want us to enjoy the lake, to enjoy nature. That's what he was all about."

"Definitely. You know, sometimes I wonder who I'd be if I hadn't known Sam."

"And? Who would you be?"

"I guess the best way to put it is that he expanded me. He made me a better person, a more thoughtful and open person."

"Me too," I say.

"Look!" Skip points up at a tree along the shoreline. "See that red-tailed hawk?"

It's dusk, but I can make out the outline of the bird he's referring to. "Yes, I see it, but how do you know it's a red-tail?"

"It's been following us since we left your house. It's strange, but ever since I was at Wilderness, I've been seeing red-tailed hawks. Those were the only feathers I ever collected, so if Sam wanted to show me he was still around, that's the bird he'd use."

"You think that's Sam?" I say, surprised.

"I think it's possible. I also had a great horned owl make a nest in a tree right outside my window at boarding school. Owls and hawks were his two favorite birds, so I feel like he's been sending them to me as a sign that he's still around. I'm no expert on such things, but the sheer number of sightings I've had is difficult to ignore. What about you? Have you had any sightings of Sam or felt him around you?"

"Sometimes I think I feel him around me. It's like the energy in the room will suddenly change. And right after he left, I started seeing this black wolf. I've seen it now like half a dozen times and always during the day. The only other person who's seen it is my mom. And I know I'm not imagining it, because I've also seen its footprints."

"A wolf? No way, that is awesome. Wolves were even more sacred to Sam than birds. So, do you think it's possible that his spirit could inhabit more than one animal at the same time?"

"With Sam anything is possible. That way he could watch over both of us at the same time." I tell Skip about our shamanic ritual and how I had a vision of a wolf licking him.

"Wow. What do you think that means?"

"I didn't fully understand at the time, but I'm pretty sure Sam was showing me forgiveness."

Skip smiles and nods. "I'd like to believe that, but it's tough. He'd definitely still be with us if I hadn't brought him that stupid belt."

"I don't think that's necessarily true. From everything I've read, it sounds like we die when we're supposed to die. It's like we've prearranged it all. I believe Sam's soul's journey in this lifetime was over. He'd accomplished what he was here to do, and for his soul to expand any further he knew he needed a new body and a new set of circumstances."

"Where are you getting all this from?"

"Books, YouTube videos of people who've had near-death experiences, podcasts of those who channel people who've crossed over. It's all out there, and the stories are nearly identical.

This is something I'd been studying for years. But then Sam passed, and I dismissed it all. I couldn't make sense of it in the context of *his* death."

"And now?"

"I'm back to being a believer. I don't know what Sam's soul gained in this lifetime, but I know my soul learned a lot from him. He's the reason I was motivated to learn about this stuff, about what happens between lives. He was the one who was always trying to get me to see the bigger picture, to believe and listen in my inner wisdom, and to see that we are connected to every living being on the planet, that we are all one."

Skip nods and doesn't say anything for a while. "He was always telling me all that, too. But I didn't take it as seriously as you did. Honestly, it was a lot to take in. But I think I'm ready to learn more. Could you send me some of these links? It sounds like they might help me better accept his death. It was wonderful to have your family embrace and forgive me, but I'm still a long way off from forgiving myself."

"Sure, I'd be happy to send you links. But just remember, we're all a work in progress or else we wouldn't be here. I sound like I've got this stuff wired, but trust me, I don't."

"I'll try to keep that in mind."

We continue chatting as we cruise around the lake, and everywhere we go, the red-tailed hawk follows us, from branch to branch along the shore. The longer I'm with Skip, the more comfortable I feel. Part of me doesn't want to leave him tomorrow, but realistically, I know that once his friends know he's in town, they'll be all over him, and that's as it should be. The important thing is that we've reconnected; and going forward, I'll work hard to keep us connected. I can tell it's been hard for him that his parents moved so far away and to a place he feels no connection with. I can't imagine my parents leaving Crystal Lake, much less Minnesota.

When we get to the dock, Skip offers to help me load my camping stuff into the Volvo. When we're finished, I get him bedding from the closet and meet him in the den. "You don't have to hang with us tonight. I'm sure you're dying to see your friends, and I know they'll all be psyched to have you back," I say.

"Thanks, but I'm exactly where I want to be," he says.

I smile. "Me too."

The rest of the family eventually joins us in the den, and soon we are all reminiscing about Sam: the funny pranks he pulled, the weird shit he did, sayings he had, and of course, his endless Inuit stories. Rather than it being painful to hear, it's uplifting to remember just how deeply he touched all of our lives in the short time he was here. It's almost like he knew his time would be limited, and he made the most of it.

I'm the first to excuse myself, at around eleven. I'm exhausted, and I'm picking up Julie at six in the morning and don't want to be drowsy for the long ride ahead of us. When I go to hug Skip goodnight, he whispers that he'd like to have a quick word with me and then follows me into the hall.

He rests his arms on either side of my shoulder and looks me straight in the eyes and starts to tear up. "Thanks for everything. This has been one of the best nights of my life. Just being back in your house with your family has made me feel centered again. I'll never lose touch with you again, promise. Maybe you'll even come visit me in Boulder. You'd like it there. It's the perfect place for a Bean."

I laugh. "That would be awesome." He reaches his arms around me and gives me a very big, strong hug. Instantly my body is tingling, like it's been electrified with a positive charge.

THIRTEEN

My alarm goes off at 5:30 in the morning, and I'm in such a deep sleep that it rings for almost a full minute before I'm awake enough to reach over and shut it off. Since Sam died, I've been sleeping either very little or very lightly, or a combination of the two. But last night I slept so soundly that I feel as if I'm coming out of a long hibernation. I take a freezing-cold shower just to try and regain consciousness, which is a bummer because it's the last warm shower I'll have for the next five days.

On my way out, I pass the den, and see Skip sprawled on the sofa. His curly auburn hair is spread out on the pillow rather than in a ponytail, and he's wearing a blue-and-gold Chasten T-shirt. It's a funny combination, this prepster/hipster look. But either way, he looks so hot, I seriously want to jump him. But, of course, I refrain. I still believe he's my destiny, but if that's true, then I have to trust that it will all unfold exactly when it's supposed to.

I pull into Julie's driveway and see her waiting for me on their front porch. I help her load her stuff in the trunk, and we both get settled in the front seat.

"Ready?" I ask.

"So ready I can't tell you," she says.

"You look awful. Why are your eyes all puffy and bloodshot?"

"My sister had her birthday party last night, and they stayed up until like five. I don't think I slept more than an hour at most. I want to kill her."

"No problem. There's a pillow in the back, and that seat goes completely flat. I've got the address set on my phone, and I'm totally wide awake. So, lie back and relax so you'll be well rested by the time we get there."

"Thanks. I promise I'll be a ton of fun after I get a few hours of sleep." She cranks the seat to the flat position and in no time at all she's out cold.

I'm actually relieved she'll be sleeping, because I'm still processing the whole Skip experience. It feels like a seismic shift has taken place in the last twelve hours, and I need to get my bearings.

Julie doesn't wake up until she hears me talking to the Itasca park ranger, who's giving me directions to our backwoods campsite, which is a five-mile hike from the closest parking lot.

"Wow, I can't believe I slept the whole way. What a shitty copilot I was," she says, wiping the sleep from her eyes.

"No problem. It was a beautiful, scenic drive, and I caught up on a bunch of podcasts." I pull into our designated parking lot. "Let's grab our backpacks and get going."

The hike takes us about two hours because we stop often to talk to other hikers along the trail who tell us about their favorite trails and picnic spots. When we arrive at our campsite, we set up our tent in a fairly flat, grassy area under a huge pine tree about thirty feet from a majestic lake. There are two lower branches that will be perfect for stringing up our food so we won't attract bears.

When we're finished, we put on our bathing suits and head down to the lake with a picnic I'd packed. It's early in the season, so we thankfully have the place pretty much to ourselves. There are a few older guys fishing, but they're on the opposite shore and they're very quiet. We lay out our towels and unpack our lunch. After I've had my first few bites of salad, I begin. "Guess who's at my house right now."

Julie gives me a curious look. "I have no idea. Who?"

"Skip."

"What? Seriously?" Julie says, her eyebrows arched. "No way. Oh my God, tell me everything."

And so, I do.

"I've actually heard of auto asphyxiation," she says. "I read about a bunch of really young kids who did that in an elementary school bathroom in Canada on one of those cloth towel dispensers. I think it's also called the choking game. But I didn't know that it was also done for sexual reasons."

"I Googled it last night before I went to sleep and was pretty shocked to find out how many deaths have been attributed to it. It's literally been going on for thousands of years in one form or another. They don't have an accurate count of the deaths, because if it's AEA, a lot of times parents or whoever will tamper with the crime scene and the body so it doesn't look like anything sexual was going on. Not sure why something sexual would be worse than a suicide, but that's our society for you."

"Doesn't it make you mad that you're just finding this out? Think how different everything would've been if you'd have understood from the start that it wasn't a suicide," Julie says.

I don't say anything for a few seconds, because I want to answer her question thoughtfully. "I've had time to think about this, and I actually think it's better that it all came out the way it did."

"Really?"

"Yes, because if Skip had come over that night or the next morning or whatever and told us what happened, we would have totally blamed him, probably even hated him, and I doubt we'd have been able to ever forgive him."

"And now?" Julie asks.

"We're all in a way better spot. I think we've all come around to the idea that Sam was a gift that we were able to enjoy for the time he was with us. We didn't lose anything. We gained from having him in our lives for the time we did. You know, I've been working really hard to turn my grief into gratitude. And now I'm choosing to be thankful rather than resentful. And I'm especially thankful to have Skip back in our lives."

"Yeah, but he's not blameless. If he hadn't brought over that belt and those instructions, Sam would still be alive."

"But he is still alive. Right? Ever since we did our shamanic ritual, I've totally believed that. I've felt him around me because I've *allowed* myself to feel him, and I've also *allowed* myself to believe that souls never really die. Would I rather have him back in his physical form as my brother? Of course, I would. But I don't have a say in that. I just have to accept that he was here in his physical form for the period he was supposed to be. And now I guess he's anywhere he wants to be—in a wolf, in a red-tailed hawk, wherever. He's moved on, and I need to, also."

"I'm sure you're right. I mean, I know you are. I guess I'm just surprised you can be so clear-headed about it all. It would take me a while to be as accepting toward Skip as you seem to be. How did the rest of your family react—or don't they know yet?"

"They all know and they were beyond amazing. Seriously. I'm so proud of them. We've gone from a family divided to a family united. How many times does a death in a family cause that to happen?"

"I would guess never. So, how does he look? Do you still have a crush on him?" she says.

I don't even try to deny it. "His energy is so like Sam's but, well, he's super hot. I didn't think he could get any more good-looking, but he did." I grin.

"How long is he staying?"

"Just till Wednesday."

"He's only here for a few days, he's staying with you, you have a mad crush on him, and yet you're here with me? Have you lost your mind? This park isn't going anywhere, and neither am I. You should have told me. We could have rescheduled. I would've been fine with that."

"I'm exactly where and with whom I want to be. And, as far as Skip, well, in the words of P. T. Barnum, 'You should always leave them wanting more.'"

Julie laughs, and we simultaneously fall backwards onto our towels.

She reaches over and grabs my hand. "BFFs," she says.

I squeeze her hand. "Always and forever," I say.

A NOTE ON AUTO ASPHYXIATION AND
AUTOEROTIC ASPHYXIATION FOR TEENS

What led me to write this book was the death of my best friend's son, Brendan Flynn, at the age of twelve. Like Sam, his death appeared to be a suicide, and it took years for the truth to finally emerge. Practicing auto asphyxiation and autoerotic asphyxiation is always life-threatening. There is no way to do it safely. Don't believe your peers if they try to convince you otherwise. If you hear or believe that peers are engaging in this practice, immediately report it to an adult. You could save a life.

A NOTE ON AUTO ASPHYXIATION AND
AUTOEROTIC ASPHYXIATION FOR ADULTS

Auto asphyxiation, also known as the "choking game," "blackout game," "pass-out game," "scarf game," "space monkey," "suffocation roulette," and other names, is defined by the CDC as self-strangulation or strangulation by another person with the hands or a noose to achieve a brief euphoric state caused by cerebral hypoxia. Though exact numbers are difficult to know due to inaccurate underreporting (often such deaths are ruled suicides or of undetermined intent), it is estimated that between 5 and 10 percent of the US population has participated in this dangerous activity. It has been labeled the "good kids' drug" because a majority of the publicized deaths occurred in high-achieving children. Most of those who practice it are youths between the ages of six and nineteen. Often it results in fatality.

To prevent such dangerous practices, parents, caretakers, and physicians should be on the lookout for evidence on a child or teen's skin. Purple spots, usually on the neck or eyelids, called petechiae, indicate hemorrhaging caused by this practice. Other physical signs include neck lacerations, unexplained headaches, and disorientation or confusion after time spent alone. It's equally important to monitor the internet and YouTube activity of your children, as YouTube alone contains more than five thousand videos of self-injury and self-harm techniques. YouTube has also been found to contribute to normalizing auto asphyxiation, making it seem like a fun activity that most teens should try at some point.

ACKNOWLEDGMENTS

At the top of my list in every category imaginable, I'd like to thank Rich, who has been my loving companion, guiding star, and greatest champion in every wild endeavor I've dreamed up since he discovered me in a bar in Cozumel, Mexico, some thirty-plus years ago. I'd also like to thank our kids, Max, Shane, Hunter, and Skylar, who supported my writing while never once, in the eighteen years it took me to complete this, asking the question that I'm sure was on all their minds: "Will you ever finish your novel?"

To my early readers, Mary Treyz, Iva Peele, Beth Golde, Martina Sternfeld, and Daniel Ranger, thank you for enthusiastically supporting my story and my writing when I was just beginning this adventure. I'm especially grateful to Lisa Edmondson, who introduced me to Jennie Nash, book coach extraordinaire, who miraculously aided me in transforming an unwieldy, incoherent manuscript into a novel I could be proud of in just a few short months.

An enormous thanks to my wonderful team at Greenleaf Book Group: Dan Pederson, Tyler LeBleu, Jessica Choi, Jay Hodges, Elizabeth Brown, Neil Gonzalez, Kristine Peyre-Ferry, Olivia McCoy, O'Licia Parker Smith, and Justin Branch.

FOR FURTHER READING

I am forever indebted to the following authors whose books have inspired, informed, and provided source material for this novel. I hope readers who are interested in these subjects will explore these titles.

Spiritual and Life-After-Death Sources

All books by Dolores Cannon

All books by Elisabeth Kübler-Ross

Animal Speak, The Spiritual & Magical Powers of Creatures Great and Small by Ted Andrews

Awakening to the Spirit World: The Shamanic Path of Direct Revelation by Sandra Ingerman & Hank Wesselman

Broken Open: How Difficult Times Can Help Us Grow by Elizabeth Lesser

Conversations with God, Books 1, 2, and 3 by Neale Donald Walsch

Death Without Fear by Tony Stubbs

Feeling Is the Secret by Neville Goddard

From Here to Eternity: Traveling the World to Find the Good Death
by Caitlin Doughty

Good Mourning by Elizabeth Meyer

Happier Endings: A Meditation on Life and Death by Erica Brown

Man's Search for Meaning by Viktor E. Frankl

Oneness by Rasha

The Power of Awareness by Neville Goddard

Proof of Heaven: A Neurosurgeon's Journey into the Afterlife
by Eben Alexander, M.D.

Shadows on a Path by Abdi Assadi

The Untethered Soul: The Journey Beyond Yourself
by Michael A. Singer

Waking Up: A Guide to Spirituality Without Religion by Sam Harris

Inuit Sources

*Amerindian Rebirth: Reincarnation Belief Among North American
Indians and Inuit* edited by Antonia Mills and Richard Slobodin

Ethnology of the Ungava District by Lucien M. Turner

Inuit Folktales collected by Knud Rasmussen

Sacred Hunt: A Portrait of the Relationship between Seals and Inuit
by David F. Pelly

Writing on Ice: The Ethnographic Notebooks of Vilhjalmur Stefansson
edited and introduced by Gísli Pálsson

AUTHOR Q&A

Q: The book presents a unique blend of the spiritual and detective genres. What inspired you to bring these two together in *Winter of the Wolf?*

A: My favorite novels are ones in which there is soul growth from the beginning of the book to the end, and I love a good mystery. This story seemed like the perfect platform for such a story arc. I also wanted to show that our spiritual growth is not always a straight line. Bean believes Sam didn't commit suicide, but she also has doubts along the way. This is normal and a part of the process. The trick is to push through.

Q: Do you have a favorite character in the story? If so, what is it about this character that you most appreciate?

A: I love Bean's fortitude and perseverance. She continues to listen and act on her gut instincts despite the overwhelming amount of evidence suggesting that her assumptions about Sam's innocence had to be misinformed. I wish that when I was fifteen, I would have had the wherewithal to truly be myself and not be so concerned with what others thought of me. In my mind, that makes Bean a real hero.

Q: What was your favorite chapter to write in *Winter of the Wolf* and why?

A: Chapter Twelve was my favorite because it showed the deep growth and wisdom that was gained by each of the family members in their personal journeys of self-discovery since Sam's passing; these ultimately allowed them to fully embrace rather than blame Skip for the role he played in Sam's death. The family members were all able to move from grief to gratitude, and that is the foundation of my novel. I can only hope it feels as gratifying to read as it was to write and that my readers take away something profound from this that they can apply in their own lives when the time comes—and it will come!

Q: On the other side of the spectrum, were there any chapters that were particularly challenging for you to write? If so, can you share what it was about these parts of the story that challenged you?

A: Chapter Two was by far the most difficult chapter to write, both from a technical perspective as well as an emotional one. To understand car crash scenarios and their effects on passengers, I watched lots of gruesome videos. For my myriad medical questions, I consulted with a relative who is an EMT and did many Google searches on the subject. It was tough to learn exactly what Sam's body would look like after such a death and how long the medical personnel would presumably spend trying to resurrect him. And because this story is based loosely on a friend's child's death, it was especially horrible for me to imagine what she and her family must have experienced in the aftermath of his death.

But the hardest part of all was putting myself in Bean's head and trying to imagine what she was seeing and experiencing after finding Sam's body. As much as I wanted to shield her from the experience, I knew she had to be in the thick of it, experiencing everything firsthand. It was emotionally draining to construct and deconstruct all the necessary elements, and I shed more than a few tears in the process.

Q: Bean and her family's depression and grief feel very real. Is this something you've had to experience in your life or helped someone else through?

A: I have numerous family members who've been diagnosed with depression, and I've lost many friends to suicide. As depression is now a nationwide epidemic, I think we all bear a responsibility to learn as much as we can about it so that we're able to see that suicide is far from a "selfish" act, as so many unfairly judge it. It would seem obvious that if someone is in so much pain that ending their lives seems like the only viable solution, they have no ability to look outside themselves to see how their actions might affect others. One of my favorite books on the subject is William Styron's *Darkness Visible*. It helps one understand the mind frame of those with serious depression.

As far as grief goes, I doubt there's anyone who's reached a certain age who's been spared. It's part of the life cycle and it's what makes us human.

Q: At the end of the novel, we see Bean and her friends and family forgive Skip for the role he played in Sam's death. Is this true to you and your friends' real-life experiences?

A: Yes. Holding on to hatred, resentment, or anger will consume you, while forgiveness sets your soul free and allows your heart to open a little wider. Forgiveness is not a one-time act; it's something you have to do over and over again. In the end, it's not about the other person, it's about you.

Q: In the notes after the last chapter, you reveal that your friend's son died in a very similar manner to Sam. What about that experience inspired you to begin writing?

A: When my friend's son died, because of the way it happened, everyone assumed it was a suicide. People immediately placed blame on the family (Why didn't they get him to a therapist or put him on medication, etc.?) and on the victim (What a terribly selfish act). I wanted readers to think about the inappropriate and hurtful words that are often spoken in the aftermaths of suicides.

But what really inspired me was that my friend, this boy's mother, never wavered in her belief that her son did not choose to end his life. Call it what you want, but our instincts, intuition, or gut feelings about something are a true gift and should never be ignored. If something doesn't feel right or sit well with you, you owe it to yourself to honor that feeling and act accordingly.

Q: Throughout the novel, both Bean and Sam hold a deep belief in the importance of the connection between people and the natural world. Is this a belief you share?

A: I do. Every indigenous culture I've studied felt this connection, and then in subsequent cultures, this connection has been eroded. Nature is fascinating and perfect, with everything having a purpose and a role, though I find the role of humans much more difficult to understand! I enjoy learning about things such as the doctrine of signatures or seeing movies like *The Biggest Little Farm*, both of which illustrate the magical way that nature works. But I worry that while our Earth has been wonderfully resilient thus far, we're now exceeding its carrying capacity and ability to fully recover from our exploitive practices.

Q: Your knowledge of the spiritual and Inuit practices seems significant. Did that knowledge lead you to the story, or did the story lead you to that knowledge?

A: My spiritual leanings and curiosity about reincarnation started when I was very young. Like Bean, I attended many funerals with my mother, and I often felt the deceased's spirit in the room. I also frequently saw the ghost of an older woman dressed in Victorian attire whenever I spent the night at a certain friend's home. Thankfully, my mother and a few other key friends believed me and supported and encouraged me to learn more about the spirit world.

My interest in the Inuit happened much like Sam's did. I watched *Nanook of the North* in grade school and instantly felt a deep connection to them and to all Indigenous peoples; I believe this has to do with a past life.

Also, years ago, I encountered a deer frozen into the surface of a lake, and for a reason that I did not fully understand, something profound happened and I began to see how I could connect the tragic incident that happened to my friend's son—which she and I were both struggling to make sense of at the time—with my spiritual beliefs. I believe my knowledge of and interest in these two areas helped me see this connection and hear this story.

Q: The final chapters send a surprising and important message to readers about auto asphyxiation. What other message do you hope readers will take away from your book?

A: I hope my readers and all humans, for that matter, start to think differently about the way we treat death, both from an ecological and an emotional point of view. As stated in my novel, cremation and embalming, at least the way they've been practiced in the United States since the Civil War, are both

WINTER OF THE WOLF

horrific from an environmental standpoint. We are energy, and as such, according to the first law of thermodynamics, we cannot be created or destroyed but can only be transferred or changed from one form to another. At the time of one's death, our soul separates from our material bodies, so focusing on one's body shell or ashes seems senseless.

From an emotional perspective, I'd really like to see loved ones moving from a place of grief to one of gratitude. As Helen Keller so eloquently said, "What we once enjoyed and deeply loved we can never lose, for all that we love deeply becomes part of us." It's up to survivors to keep their loved ones alive by remembering them and passing on their stories. I would encourage anyone with an interest in this area to read some of the books I sourced. Whether the data comes from studies, those who've had near-death experiences, or those who've undergone past-life regression therapy, the information is much the same and impossible to ignore.

Q: In writing this novel, did you learn anything new about yourself or the people who inspired the story?

A: I learned perseverance! Eighteen years, even part-time, is a long time to stick with any project and I'm sure there were those around me who believed this novel would never make it to print, and I can't blame them. But I never wavered in my conviction that this story needed to be told and I was the one who needed to tell it. The voices in my head would have it no other way!

Q: You have worked as the board president of the Wolf Conservation Center. How has this work impacted your writing of *Winter of the Wolf*?

A: Like Sam, I've always been drawn to wildlife, and I understood from a young age that one of my roles in this lifetime was to be a voice for the wild things on our planet. For a long time, I saw no connection between this novel and my work on behalf of wolves. Then, about a year ago, a black wolf began appearing in my dreams, and I knew that it was trying to tell me something. Finally, it hit me just how alike Sam and wolves are; Sam was bullied and misunderstood, and so are wolves. I have a bumper sticker that reads "Little Red Riding Hood Lied," which leads to quite interesting discussions. This fairytale (and so many others like it), originally intended to warn children to be cautious of strangers, instead led people to have an unwarranted fear of wolves. When I saw that I could use my novel to help set the record straight by sprinkling in a few facts about these largely misunderstood apex predators, I pounced! I believe it's important to always try to listen to our inner voices and pay attention to our dreams. There are always lessons there if you are open to receiving and deciphering them.

Q: How do you get in the mood to write? Is there anything in particular that helps you stay focused? Do you have any writing rituals, for example?

A: I start my writing sessions by lighting a candle and incense, and then I write down three things that I'm appreciative of and three things I hope to accomplish with my writing that day. I also like to take a few deep breaths to settle into whatever workspace I happen to be occupying. Because this novel took eighteen years to complete, I've worked in many different locations and environments. But these simple rituals always center me and help me feel rooted no matter where I am or how long I have to write.

Q: Did you receive any advice that helped you through your writing journey? What advice would you pass along to other aspiring authors?

A: Early on, I was in a few writing groups, but I found they didn't work well for me. I had very limited time to write, and I didn't want to spend the precious time I did have reading and critiquing others' writing. But this meant I was writing in a bubble and making the same mistake many first-time novelists make, which is to put everything but the kitchen sink in the book! Recently, someone asked if I'd be interested in speaking to her friend who was a book coach. I hadn't even known such a job existed. Long story short, I hired her, and it was the best decision I ever made.

My first assignment with my book coach was to write down why I was writing the novel. It's such an obvious step, and yet it wasn't anything I'd thought through with any clarity, which explained why my story was meandering all over the place. Once I understood what my purpose was, I developed an outline, and then the structure and chapters quickly fell into place.

I found that after working in a bubble for all those years, I really thrived when I was given strict deadlines, and my book coach's critique of my chapters proved invaluable. She would often say, "This is a funny story, but if it doesn't deepen the reader's understanding of a character or move the plot along, it has to go."

Q: Do you have ideas for a second novel or book? If so, what can you tell us about it?

A: Part of me wants to follow Bean in her journey into adulthood to see how the death of Sam ultimately changes her and informs her life decisions. I also wonder if she and Skip have a future and if there was something going on with his family that hasn't yet been explored. However, another part of me is ready to let these characters go and pursue a project that is much more fun and lighter. I guess book sales will ultimately help me make this decision! All I know for sure is that there is nothing that makes me happier than writing—except maybe wolves!

ABOUT THE AUTHOR

Martha Hunt Handler grew up in northern Illinois dreaming about wolves and has always understood that her role in this lifetime is to tell stories and be a voice for nature. She has been an environmental consultant, a magazine columnist, an actress, and a polar explorer, among other occupations. She has also driven across the country in an 18-wheeler and been a grand-prize winner of *The Newlywed Game*.

Soon after she and her family relocated from Los Angeles to South Salem, New York, she began to hear wolves in her backyard. This was the start of her twenty-plus-year career as an advocate for wolves at the Wolf Conservation Center. When not up near the wolves and her rescue pups, she can be found in New York City with her husband and four adult children.

This is her first novel but definitely not her last.

Visit Martha at: marthahunthandler.com

All book sales proceeds received by the author will go to the Wolf Conservation Center (nywolf.org), a nonprofit environmental organization with a mission to 1) educate the public about the vital role that wolves, as keystone predators, play in our ecosystems, 2) advocate on behalf of wolves by equipping the public with pertinent knowledge and tools, and 3) participate in the recovery plans of the two most critically endangered animals in North America: the red wolf and the Mexican gray wolf.